I0587379

THE RISE OF THE GODDESS

BOOKS IN CHURCH OF THE SEER

The Dark Reveal
The Reign of the Dragon

CHURCH OF THE SEER

THE RISE OF THE GODDESS

KENYA FOUCH

BOOKLOGIX
Alpharetta, Georgia

ISBN: 978-1-6653-1013-0 - Paperback
eISBN: 978-1-6653-1014-7 - eBook

Library of Congress Control Number: 2025910628

♾This paper meets the requirements of ANSI/NISO Z39.48-1992
(Permanence of Paper)

0 5 2 9 2 5

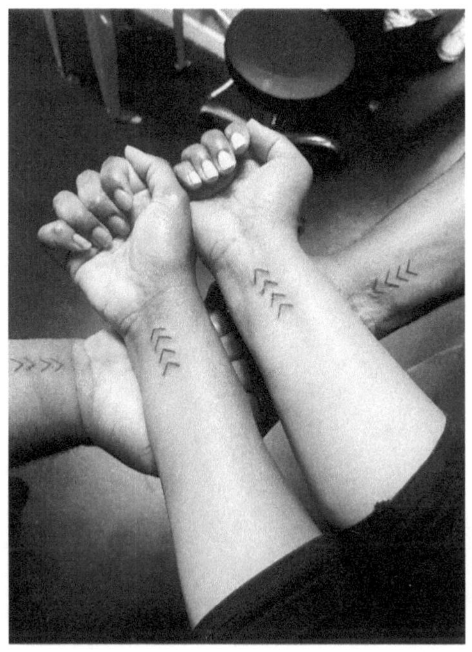

*"Now the serpent was more crafty than any other
beast of the field that the Lord God had made."*
—*Genesis 3:1 (ESV)*

CHURCH OF THE
SEER

① 1

ORIGINS

Mara struggled to control the car as they sped along the muddy road. The wipers earned their keep as the windshield fought the harsh rain paired with the occasional grimy blob that splashed up from the sinkholes in the road. The headlights provided a measure of relief but were no match for the darkness under the dense canopy of overgrown clove trees that lined the narrow path. Mara did her best to accommodate her mother, but her vision was limited and they were already traveling dangerously fast for the conditions.

"Hurry, Unimara. We mustn't be late."

"But Mama, I don't even know where we're going. And if you haven't noticed, it's raining sideways."

"Just press your pedals. I'll direct you, but you must drive faster."

Mara felt the laxity in the steering wheel as the car slid side to side. She just kept driving. "Perhaps I would if I knew what this was all about. Are you in trouble again?"

"No, Unimara, I'm not in trouble. And mind your tone, young lady."

"Please forgive me, Mama, but neither you nor Papa have spoken to me since my engagement, and now, suddenly, there's someone you want me to meet?"

"No, dear, there is someone who wants to meet *you*."

"That's what I just said."

"You will thank me later."

"If this is about Kobe . . ."

"Oh please, if Kabeyesi had the brains to match his ambitions—"

"Mama, Kobe is a brilliant man, and he will be my husband in three days' time. We're moving to Lagos in two weeks."

"Two weeks? Your fellowship doesn't begin until August."

"Kobe wants to move now so we won't be distracted when our work begins, and I happen to agree with him."

"And when were you planning to inform your family?"

"When you started speaking to me again!"

The car mercifully broke through into a clearing and Mara was able to see lights through a large iron gate that stood in front of a three-story mansion with a massive garden inside a circular driveway. Two gaudy statues flanked the gated entrance, each a black lion carved from onyx standing on a golden sphere.

"Fine. But none of that matters right now. Slow down. There. The gate, just between the figures."

As Mara slowed, the gate began to open. She cautiously guided the vehicle off the dirt road, through the opening, and around the garden. The contrast between the erratic road and the smooth pavers made her feel uneasy, as if she were a mouse unaware of the looming body-crushing pinch of a trap.

"What is this place? I don't remember seeing this on any of our other trips to Pemba."

"It's new. I understand it was constructed for a singular purpose."

"What purpose is that?"

"You, dear."

"Mama, please. Stop being cryptic. Just tell me what this is."

"You have been chosen."

"Chosen for what, exactly?"

"Purpose."

Mara slowly pressed the brakes, and the car came to a halt right in front of a sweeping staircase leading to ceiling-height double doors. She wiped her eyes and intently turned toward her mother. "What purpose, Mama?"

Mara was becoming justifiably apprehensive, and her mother feared she might impulsively drive away. "He has selected you as his Nija Takatifu."

"A vessel? Mama, what kind of vessel? And who is *he*?"

"He goes by many names, but we call him Mungu Jua."

Mara quickly leaned back and rolled her eyes before releasing an acerbic snicker. "Ahh. Very creative. It seems ironic, though, that I would meet the sun god in the middle of the night during a thunderstorm. Perhaps Shango was unavailable." She flailed her arms in a show of derision.

"Don't be sassy, Unimara."

"Mama, I am a scientist. I have neither the time nor the interest to engage in your tribal delusions."

"Please, Unimara, I've already told you more than I should've."

"You haven't told me anything."

"I've told you all I can. That's how he wants it. He has chosen you, now you must choose him."

"If I am to choose him, why are we in such a hurry?"

"The migrations have already begun, dear. We are grateful for his patience."

"I don't understand."

"Theirs not to reason why, theirs but to do and die."

"Mama . . ."

"Nenda, chombo chenye heshima!" (*Go, noble vessel!*)

Mara let out as loud a sigh as she could manage and slowly opened the door. As she stepped out of the vehicle the rain suddenly subsided, and the clouds were swept away as if by the brushstroke of a master artist. The clear sky beamed light from a full moon surrounded by twinkling stars that provided a perfect illustration of Taylor's tune. Mara pulled her hair back into a ponytail and secured it with a small pink scrunchie. As she started to walk up the stairs, her mother lowered the passenger window and whispered, "I'll be here whenever you get back."

Mara turned her head and continued to climb the stairs, marveling at the sheer size of the facility. As she approached the front door, she was tempted to knock but decided to look for a doorbell instead. Before she could look away, the doors opened and she was greeted by two large women, both with one hand on a door and the other hand holding a large spear. Mara slowly walked through the doors and was astounded by the aesthetics of the large entry room. The floor was white marble and there were two staircases, one on each side of the room, that led to a balcony stretching the length of the area.

The room was full of clay and bronze sculptures, colorful paintings, and ancient artifacts in glass cases. Mara was drawn to a large display case with handwritten works by Cheikh Anta Diop and Francis Allotey. She was familiar with the writings but had never seen original prints. As she allowed herself to be impressed by the display, she heard a gentle greeting from behind her.

"I thought you might appreciate the writings of the physicists."

Mara abruptly stepped back before turning to face the source of the greeting. She fully intended to speak but was unable to form words. Standing before her, in a gentle pose with his hands behind his back, was a man that her mind immediately interpreted as physical perfection. He was tall, slightly more than two meters, with flawless brown skin and jet-black hair, not one out of place. She could see the form of his body even through his modest garments. His aura was the culmination of a pairing she had never seen in a human, absolute power and genuine humility. Mara cleared her throat and hoped her words would come out.

"Ahem, yes, I studied physics at Caleb in Nigeria. I've read everything Diop has written."

"Very impressive. Beauty and brains, a lethal combination." His voice was clear, pleasant, and strong. Mara was irritated that she wanted to impress him. She trusted him and her inhibitions began to fade. She felt safe. She felt unworthy.

"I try to use my powers for good." She chuckled awkwardly and regretted speaking. He smiled.

"Please excuse my lack of manners. My name is Nyambe. I am honored that you have accepted my invitation this evening."

Mara was reminded that she was in the presence of a total stranger, and her skepticism returned along with her stubbornness.

"I would introduce myself, but it seems you already know me."

"I do."

Mara found his quiet confidence to be both annoying

and irresistible. "How is it that you have come to know me, Nyambe?" As she spoke, she removed the scrunchie and let her hair fall to her shoulders.

"I know many things, Unimara, as do you. We know what we should, and we learn what we must."

"Why have you summoned me here? My mother was very secretive in transit."

"Ah, yes, right to business. You certainly are as advertised." Nyambe smiled again.

"That isn't an answer." Mara smirked, and was instantly disgusted at herself for flirting.

"Very well." Nyambe's countenance became stoic and his mannerisms more deliberate. "Unimara, you are chosen among women. You are the vessel. You are my vessel." He reached for Mara's hand. When he touched her, she took a deep breath and realized she was no longer in control of her mind.

"Yes, my lord. I am compelled." Mara was aware of her words, though they didn't come from her own thoughts.

Nyambe pulled Mara close and kissed her. "Do you surrender?"

Mara placed her hands on Nyambe's face and kissed him. "Yes, my lord. I surrender." Mara was aware of her actions, though involuntary.

Nyambe kissed her again. "Do you desire?"

Mara began to breathe faster, and she felt feverish. She kissed him with joy and fury. "Yes, my lord. I desire."

"My honored vessel, you have found favor with me. I will fill you with pleasure and passion and you will conceive in your womb. He will be endowed with the great powers of the darkness at the center of the sun. Do you yield?"

Mara was overcome with emotion and began to weep.

"Yes, my lord. I yield. Let it be to me according to your word." Nyambe swept Mara off her feet and lifted her into his arms. He quickly and calmly ascended the stairs into his chambers, where he gave her incessant pleasure all that night until sunrise. As the sun peered over the horizon into the large windows, Mara fell into the deepest sleep she had ever known. She was awakened the following evening in her bed at her mother's house in Tanga.

Mara was tempted to believe her experience with the sun god Nyambe was only a dream until she began to hear the voices with greater clarity and frequency. She realized she had been groomed for this moment since her youth, and her thoughts transitioned to the child she now knew to be a part of a baleful plan.

(**2**)

MIAMI

Ukweli sat at his desk, staring at the computer screen. There was movement, but he hadn't been able to confirm the numbers the intel was reporting. If Imperium had a final stronghold here in Miami, it was worth calling the team in. No need worrying everyone if it was just a few torqs, though. The Seers had been extremely efficient in destroying the remnants of Imperium all over the world, and now a single lodge house had been discovered in Miami. If this was indeed the final blow to Imperium, Ukweli wanted it done right. He wanted it done completely. He wanted it done forever.

Ukweli was now six months past his thirtieth birthday. Thirty is the new twenty, and Ukweli was in great shape, but the life of a Seer ages men like dogs and Ukweli had been through more than most. His life as an international demon hunter had taken its toll, and he allowed himself to be excited about the mere possibility of the war coming to an end.

He watched the screen closely, looking for heat signatures. *I know you're here. I'll find you one way or another.*

"Maybe you need to take your eyes off the screen for a while." Mendoza came into the room wearing a pink two-piece bikini, long white socks with three pink stripes at the top, a teal bucket hat, and size eight rollerblades that transitioned from teal at the top to hot pink at the bottom. Her black hair was braided, the longest of which nearly reached her waist. She had arrived in Miami the week prior when she was informed of the possibility of significant Imperium mobilization there.

"I don't want to miss them. As soon as I confirm they're here, I'll call the team in."

"Listen, if Antonio says they're here, then they're here. He's plugged into this city. No one moves without him knowing about it."

"So, you think I should call everyone in?"

"No worries. I already made the call."

"What?"

"I made the call. Antonio and Trent are already here. Marianne will be here tomorrow morning."

"What about my team?"

"Well, I didn't want to involve them without talking to you first. I wasn't sure you would need them."

"If these numbers are accurate, I don't want to take any chances."

"Okay, I'll take care of it. I'll put in the call now." She pressed some buttons on her communicator.

"Thank you."

"Ukweli . . ."

He sighed. "Yes, Claire?"

"You promised me we would spend some time together on this trip."

"And we will, as soon as—"

"Nope. No more excuses. The call has been made. The team is assembling." She maneuvered toward Ukweli and leaned on the edge of the desk. "I hardly get to see you as it is. You promised me I would feel important when you got to Miami. Well, you're in Miami, and I don't feel important yet."

"I'm sorry. You're right. What do you want to do?"

"I want to go rollerblading on the strip. It's a beautiful day. It will do you good to get some sunshine on your face."

Ukweli raised an eyebrow. "Do I look like I roller-blade?"

"Fine. What do you want to do?"

Ukweli turned toward Mendoza and looked her over. He stood up, walked over to her, and put his hands on her waist. He pulled her close to him and kissed her deeply. "I'm not going rollerblading, but I could use a little exercise."

She put her arms around his neck, kissed him, and smiled. "Been waiting on that since you got here."

He lifted her up and she wrapped her legs around his waist. They kissed as he swept her off to the bedroom.

Kiera sat on the couch holding a hot cup of masala chai tea. She was in awe of the Swiss landscape, and she had grown to love the sound of the fast-flowing river just a few feet past the fence in the backyard. Life in Zurich moved at a much slower pace than she was accustomed to, but she was convinced it was best for her children. Kip had finally, mercifully, fallen asleep on a pillow and Kiera softly rubbed her tiny back with her free hand. Kip was now two and a half, and her energy resources were seemingly endless. She loved to run. She loved to cook. She loved to explore, particularly Pax's room. In fact, nothing gave Kip more pleasure than destroying something that belonged to Pax. The nanny, Mrs. Bergstrom, was in the back getting Pax bathed and ready for bed. Mrs. Bergstrom was a godsend for Kiera. Ukweli hardly trusted anyone with his children, but he knew Kiera needed help with him being gone so often. Mrs. Bergstrom's husband had been a leader in ARD-10 and was killed on a mission, so she well understood the stresses of loving a soldier. She had been able to help Kiera with the kids and with Kiera's own mental health. Most importantly, Ukweli trusted her.

Kiera desperately looked forward to the end of the war. She knew Ukweli to be a man of great focus, and in the five years since his battle with DayStar in Atlanta, his only life goal was the complete destruction of all remnants of Imperium. He owed it to Uzuri. He owed it to Kobe and Mara. He owed it to Ava. Kiera did her best to remain patient, though she wasn't always successful. She also did her best to remain silent. She was *hardly ever* successful. She wasn't Ava. Kiera refused to honor Ukweli with silence. When she had something to say, she said it.

Their marriage had been strained recently. She would never be convinced it was because she talked too much, though. Maybe it was the children. They required a lot of her attention and consumed a lot of her energy. She knew Ukweli loved her, but she had trouble adjusting to his lack of communication. Ukweli's *ability* to communicate was quite extraordinary—in several different languages, in fact—but his *unwillingness* to communicate often forced her to say things that might have been better left unsaid.

Regardless, she always looked forward to Ukweli coming

home from wherever he happened to be in the world. She genuinely missed him when he was gone. Ukweli's children adored him. Kiera did too.

JULY 3, 2050

Mendoza hopped out of the shower and grabbed a bathrobe. She tried to collect as many of her personal items from Ukweli's room as she could. Most of the Seers had an idea about their affair, but she didn't want to give them proof if they ever came looking. Her plan was to sneak out of his room quietly, an otherwise great idea thwarted by her lack of awareness. She had been so carefree that she hadn't noticed the time. When she left Ukweli's room and entered the living area, she was greeted by the entire team; Antonio, Trent, and Marianne sat on the couch while Paul, Kei, Adam, Charlotte, and Kelley sat around the table.

Kelley smiled and shook her head when Mendoza walked into the room. "You look especially radiant this morning, Mendoza." Adam chuckled.

"Thank you, Kelley." Mendoza rolled her eyes and looked away as she spoke. She kept walking.

"It's good that Ukweli's bed suits you. After all, there's nothing more important than a good night's sleep." Kelley held her hands under her chin, palms down, as if posing for a photo, and fluttered her eyelashes.

Mendoza stopped and turned toward the team. "It's not what it looks like."

Kelley snapped back. "How do you know what I think it looks like?"

"You think I'm sleeping with Ukweli."

"Well that much is obvious. I just wonder why you can't

do your dirt and then sleep in your own bed. Most street-walkers know that much."

"Well, given that you spent so much of your life living on the street, I guess you would know."

The jeers from some of the team members prompted Kelley to take a more aggressive approach. "I definitely know a slut when I see one."

"What are you trying to say, Kelley?" Mendoza took an ill-advised step toward her.

Kelley stood up. "What? Was I being too subtle?"

As Kelley started closing the distance between them, Ukweli walked into the room. He had been meeting with an informant in the café downstairs. "Hey guys, it's—" Sensing the tension, he paused and looked around the room. "Uh, what's going on?"

Kelley relented and made a sweeping motion with her hand toward Mendoza as she returned to her seat at the table. "UK, your relationships are none of my business, but it's disrespectful to flaunt it with Mongolian Barbie."

Mendoza shook her head and rolled her eyes again. "I'm Filipina."

Ukweli shifted his eyes down, back to the screen in his hand. "Kelley, quit jumping to conclusions. Besides, you're right, it's none of your business." Mendoza childishly stuck out her tongue, flipped her hair, and walked to her room.

After a few moments of awkward silence, Adam chuckled again. "I mean, it is disrespectful, like in so many ways, but I get it. Miss Thang got curves in all the right places."

"Seriously, Adam?"

"I'm just saying, bruv. Chun-Li got it going on."

"Wow, now who's being disrespectful?" They both laughed.

Charlotte spoke up. "If you boys are done with your locker room talk, what did the informant say?"

Ukweli cleared his throat. "Just about everything Antonio said was correct. It's happening this morning. They're making a full-scale assault on a church here today."

"Did they say which church?"

"No."

"Do we know how many churches?"

"It seems just one, but with their numbers, they could hit just about all of them."

Charlotte leaned up and looked at Antonio. "I thought you said a hundred."

Antonio shrugged. "I said *at least* a hundred."

Charlotte looked back at Ukweli. "And what are their actual numbers?"

"Closer to three hundred." Everyone gasped. Even Antonio was surprised.

Charlotte said, "That's impossible. There's no way they could've gathered a force that large without us knowing."

Ukweli responded, "They could if they waited until today to assemble."

Charlotte remained skeptical. "How could they plan and organize an attack that large in such a short time frame?"

Ukweli reasoned, "That would be difficult. That's why I think we should focus our attention on the arena."

Kei agreed. "Alexander said the security around the arena has been tight, with the celebrities coming in for the service."

Ukweli said, "We can't discount the possibility that many of the so-called security personnel may be Imperium men."

"That may complicate things. The possibility of innocent casualties will double." Charlotte spoke with concern in her voice.

Paul questioned, "And the Catholic Church is still not willing to postpone the event? Even with a clear understanding of the threat?"

"No. They say they have too much invested. They believe their security can hold it." Ukweli had grown increasingly frustrated with the Catholic Church and his belief that they were unwilling to accept that Alexander was in real danger.

Kelley started to gather her things. "Well, I'm going to the arena to get Alexander out of there. Killing Vasher today will be a bonus."

"Fine. Marianne, you go with Kelley. No one gets near Alexander. Charlotte and Kei, get to their communications center. An assault this large requires a massive comm system somewhere. Knock it out and see if you can find Vasher's location. The quicker we get to him, the quicker this thing will be over."

"And what about the rest of us?" Trent was eager, but regretted speaking as soon as the words came out.

"Do what Seers do. Hunt torqs."

Having served as camerlengo to Pope Incursus, it was thought that Alexander would quickly rise in rank, but the discussion among the cardinals concerning his association with the Seers was marred with pejoratives. It did, however, make him wildly popular with Gen Z and, as such, Alexander became one of the most highly sought after speakers in the country. But as his popularity rose, so did the threats.

Marianne sat on the couch in the makeshift green room on the northeast side of the arena. As she watched Alexander pace nervously back and forth, she couldn't help but become a little more anxious herself. This was

Marianne's first full-scale mission with the Seers. She had never even met the famous Captain Aseyori before this morning, and she was eager to prove to the Elite strike team that she could hold her own. She didn't speak to Kelley while they drove to the arena. She knew Kelley saw her as a noob, so she decided to let her fighting do the talking for her. But as Alexander's movements became more erratic, she couldn't contain her words.

"Sir? Are you okay?" Marianne softly placed her hand on Alexander's back.

Alexander turned quickly, startled. "Excuse me, dear. What?"

"Are you okay?"

"I am. I think."

"You're Kelley's husband. Haven't you gotten used to these situations by now?"

"You would think, but no. Where did Kelley say she was going again?"

"She went to the bathroom. She's right across the hall." Marianne was a little embarrassed and perfectly annoyed.

"Listen, you seem very nice and I'm sure you're capable. I would just be a lot more comfortable if my wife—"

There was a knock on the door. "Green room service."

Marianne spoke up. "We're fine. Thanks."

"We need to change out the liquids and the burners."

Marianne sighed, turned the deadbolt lock, and opened the door. Five large men burst into the room. Two of them held Marianne and two grabbed Alexander. The last man retrieved two pistols from his holster. He pointed one at Marianne and one at Alexander.

"Well, this was easier than I thought. Vasher will be pleased to know we were able to get to the priest. This will certainly rekindle the flames of war." He smiled.

There was a quiet hiss and the man's smile was the only portion of his face that remained. A splatter of red bloomed on the wall and the man fell to the floor. Marianne heard the sound of a blade slicing through the air, but by the time she opened her eyes, the other four men lay dead with fatal wounds on their chest or neck area. One of the bodies was headless. Then the sound, the shriek of the demons dissolving into the air. It sounded like something from a horror movie to Marianne. It sounded like fingernails on a chalkboard to Alexander. It sounded like a violin solo to Kelley.

"How did they get in?"

Marianne looked down. "I, uhh . . . I opened the door."

"After I told you not to open the door for any reason?"

"Yes. I'm sorry."

"Listen, we're at war. Wrap your mind around that right now. We can't afford mistakes. Mistakes cost lives."

The team was dressed to fit in with the parishioners attending the Fourth of July mass at the arena. All except Ukweli. Even after all this time, his face was still one of the most recognizable on the planet. It didn't matter to Ukweli, though. Imperium knew that word of a strong offensive would attract the Seers. Vasher knew Ukweli would show up, especially with Alexander appearing as the keynote that afternoon. If everything went to plan, Vasher could eliminate Ukweli and Kelley in one setting and get one step closer to returning Imperium to the glory it was due. That was, in fact, Vasher's plan all along.

Ukweli spoke into the comms. "Stay alert. Things are quiet. Much too quiet."

Kelley responded, "They just made a play for Alexander.

They were dressed as security detail. Keep your eyes on them."

"Charlotte, any luck with their comm center?"

"No, not yet. They're mimicking the television signals so we can't pinpoint their trailer. We'll have to check them one at a time."

"Get on it. Vasher wouldn't run an op this large without overseeing it himself. He has to be here."

Ukweli heard running footsteps behind him and turned to see ten men approaching. "I've got company."

"We have eyes on Aseyori. Should we enga—" The swift steel of Ukweli's blade removed his voice box before he could finish the question. Two of the men opened fire at Ukweli, spraying bullets into the wall behind him. Ukweli moved quickly and erratically, avoiding the gunfire and slashing the flesh of the assailants, smiling as the screeching sounds poured into the air.

The crowd inside the arena heard the gunshots and went into a panic. They flooded out of the arena, into the concourse area, and into the streets. There was now gunfire all over the arena as Imperium personnel, posing as event security, engaged the Seers. Antonio and Trent watched in awe as Adam and Paul sliced their way through wave after wave of torqs. In all the action, they were both tempted to draw their guns, but watching Adam and Paul move with precision with only their swords inspired the young duo to honor the traditions. They joined in the fray and were admittedly excited to fight beside the Elites. Though they were uncomfortable with the hissing, they were thrilled with the skill. It was hard to believe what they were seeing, and hearing.

Ukweli took on multiple units in the west corridor until he had to slip into the breezeway to avoid the raining gunfire.

The numbers turned out to be accurate; Ukweli had never faced this many torqs at once.

"I'm pinned down on the west side if anybody can hear me."

Ukweli noticed the gunfire moving away. He reemerged from the breezeway in time to see Kelley slicing and shooting her way toward his location. The sun was pouring in through the large glass outer shell of the arena, making Kelley look like a goddess as she was illuminated by the bright backdrop.

She slashed through the throats of three different machines before turning to call for Ukweli. "Hey, Captain, quit hiding!"

Ukweli had already emerged from the breezeway and was fighting alongside Kelley's position. He climbed the stairs lined with torqs and struck down nine machines, swinging his sword in a cross pattern combined with explosive lunges that tested his flexibility. UK slashed as he ducked under the enemy attacks and rose like a sharp-edged cyclone, spinning the blade of his sword into the flesh of his adversaries. Kelley opened fire on the last remaining few while he returned his blades to their fitting. He approached the final machine and landed a devastating punch to its abdomen followed by a jaw-breaking forearm before grabbing its chin and temple and ending with a swift twist. The loud "pop" was followed shortly by a shriek and hiss as the demon escaped into the air.

"Not too bad for a scaredy cat, huh?"

"I didn't say you were scared, UK. I said you were hiding."

"People hide because they're scared."

"You weren't scared, but they got the jump on you. You let them back you into a corner."

"All part of the plan."

"The plan to call for backup?"

"I wanted to give you a chance to make yourself useful."

"UK, jokes aside, you can't lose focus in this game for a second. I trained you myself, so I know the only way they pinned you down was because your mind was somewhere else. You're a great leader and you're the best fighter I've ever seen, but these . . . distractions . . . will cost you at some point." Kelley brushed Ukweli's left temple with her index finger.

"I'm not distracted. I just underestimated them."

"Well, get your shit together . . . sir. Who knows, I might not always be here to save you." She smiled and walked away.

Ukweli knew she was right. He never should've allowed a group of torqs to pin him down. He had been sloppy in preparation and in combat. He was fortunate to be alive. He was fortunate his team had survived. Ukweli went to the comms.

"Check in. Has anyone encountered Vasher?"

An unfamiliar voice responded. "No, Captain Aseyori. None of your goons have encountered me. Did you think I would stick around once we got word the Seers were mobilizing?"

Ukweli looked at Kelley and whispered, "How is he accessing our comms?" Kelley shrugged.

"Oh, don't feel bad, Captain. My technology is far and away superior to yours and my informants are more loyal. Of course, with your insatiable appetites, it's almost as if the game is rigged. Anyway, you guys have a pleasant summer. I'm sure I'll see you soon—or not."

"Vasher, you can't run forever."

"Oh, I'm not planning to. You'll be dead soon. I'd certainly like to kill you myself, but I fear I may have to stand in line.

Surely it won't be long before your beautiful wife learns of your extracurriculars. You're so obvious. No subtlety whatsoever."

"Don't ever mention my family."

"That's funny. Maybe if someone mentioned your family more often . . . You know what, never mind. You'll get what's coming to you."

3

HOME

JULY 6, 2050

U kweli stood at the front door of his home in Zurich. His keys were in his hand, but he was hesitant to walk in. He had just come from meeting with his physician, so he knew he had a clean bill of health. Well, mostly clean. It wasn't that he didn't trust Mendoza. She had a boyfriend in Atlanta, some rapper who wore more jewelry, and more makeup, than she did, but she insisted that she didn't sleep with him. Ukweli wasn't the jealous type, but he had always promised himself he would never take anything to Kiera. He always scheduled a visit to Dr. Eriksson before heading home just to be sure. Dr. Eriksson was thorough and, more importantly, discreet.

His affair with Mendoza wasn't important to him, he didn't think. He cared for her a great deal, but Kiera had his heart. Why was this bothering him now? Ukweli very rarely questioned himself or his team, but to walk into his house to inform Kiera he had been unsuccessful in capturing Vasher for the third time . . . He sighed and hung his head. Another mission fail. Another affair. He loved his wife and his children, but this was his most difficult transition—from Captain Ukweli Aseyori to *Daddy* and *Babe*.

Just before he summoned the courage to walk in, Kiera opened the door.

"Lot on your mind, babe?"

Ukweli smiled. "No more than usual." He leaned in and kissed her. "Quite the sight for sore eyes." He dropped his large duffel near the small table by the door. "I really hit the jackpot with you."

"And don't you ever forget it." They laughed and hugged.

"Where are the sprouts?"

"They're with Mrs. Bergstrom at the park for fresh air. They'll be along soon."

"Whoa. Does this mean I'm all alone with my wife? After such a difficult mission, I'm quite vulnerable to all methods of seduction."

Kiera smirked. "When have I ever had to seduce you, UK?"

Ukweli shrugged. "The apartment in Atlanta."

Kiera rolled her eyes and smiled. "Okay, other than that?"

"It doesn't matter. I just want to hear you try. Give me your best game."

Kiera paused for a few seconds. "You wanna?"

"Works for me." Ukweli grabbed Kiera's hand and led her to the bedroom.

Ukweli sat in his home office in the basement. There were three large screens, each showing a grainy video feed from team members: Kelley and Alexander, Paul and Kei, and a split screen with Adam on the top half and Charlotte on the bottom. The team, led by Kelley, requested a unit meeting with Ukweli. This was a rare occurrence. In fact, the only other unit meeting request during Ukweli's leadership came in Rome, just after Pax was born.

Ukweli looked into the faces on the screens. He trusted these people explicitly. He had no problem putting his life in their hands. He had gone to battle with each of them on multiple occasions. They were his family. He knew them well enough to know what this was about.

"Ukweli, we have concerns about . . . your focus." Paul hesitated. He had grown up with Ukweli in Islington and was his sparring partner at Highgate. He knew Ukweli as well as anyone. He had never known Ukweli to lack focus for a split second, and he suddenly wondered if the meeting was a good idea.

"UK, you gotta get rid of that girl." Kelley very often lacked tact.

Alexander cleared his voice. "Please allow me to clarify Kelley's thoughts, sir."

"I don't need you to clar—"

"Kelley, dear, please. Ukweli, we greatly admire Mendoza for what she has been through and how she has contributed to your cause. She is efficient manning the comms and I've been told she is quickly progressing in her training. Which is more than I can say for myself indeed. There is, however, the issue of the carnal nature of your relationship that we fear has clouded your judgment as the unit has sought to bring an end to this seemingly endless series of engagements with Vasher. It appears that as your feelings for her have grown, perhaps your resolve has . . ."

"My resolve has what, Alexander?" Ukweli asked the question with his eyes, looking directly into the camera. His voice was deep and clear and confrontational in a way that made everyone, even Kelley, uneasy. Ukweli was generally such a pleasant person that it was easy to forget he was a highly trained killer with a dark side in development since his youth. The entire team was reminded in a single moment that this "special assembly" was not to be taken lightly. Alexander tried to regain his composure but couldn't summon the words. So, he just sat silently.

"Look, I don't care about you and Mendoza," Charlotte interjected. "I'm just tired of chasing Vasher all over the world. The longer he lives, the greater the chance of Imperium rebuilding, and I refuse to start this war from square one."

"Thank you for your honesty, Charlotte. You know I want Vasher dead. You know I want the war to end. We'll get him. Trust me. Anything else?"

There was only silence as the team members signed off one by one until only Charlotte remained on the screen.

"Was there something more, Charlotte?"

"UK, permission to speak freely."

"Of course."

"Mendoza is in love with you."

"I'm in love with my wife. Mendoza is in a relationship. There's nothing to worry about."

"Sir, your divided love interests in the past have had a purpose. Ava and Kiera served very different roles in your life, and you needed them both. I fear that Mendoza will only serve as a distraction. Her heart will continue to demand more of your attention. There's no way it can end well."

"I appreciate your concern. I really do. Please trust that I'm in complete control of the situation."

"Yes, sir." Charlotte reluctantly signed off and the screens turned black with a rotating white Church of the Seer insignia on the middle screen.

Ukweli climbed the basement stairs and entered the living

room just as Kip and Pax burst through the front door with Mrs. Bergstrom closely following.

"Daddy!" Kip jumped into her father's arms and Pax stood beside him, waiting his turn to be embraced. Ukweli kissed Kip three times on the cheek and twirled her around before softly placing her on the floor.

"What a beautiful dress, Kipaji! Did you wear that to the park?"

"Yes, Daddy."

Mrs. Bergstrom calmly strolled by and leaned in for Ukweli to kiss her on the cheek. "She insisted. Who am I to denounce such an audacious fashion statement?"

Ukweli smiled and turned his attention to Pax, who was still standing in front of his father, patiently waiting to be acknowledged. Ukweli looked down at Pax. He seemed to have grown six inches since he last saw him. He immediately began to regret the time he spent away from him. *All of this is for you*, he thought. Ukweli saluted Pax, who quickly stood at attention and returned the salute. They began a series of handshakes unique to the two of them: shake, rotate, slide, backhand three times, hang ten, fist bump. Kiera had once asked why there was no explosion after the fist bump. Ukweli explained to her, and Pax, that there is chaos in an explosion and he was trained to maintain control. The fist bump, he said, represented the containment of the explosion. The ultimate symbol of control. Torqs thrive in chaos. Seers eliminate torqs, and chaos, through control.

He scooped Pax up into his arms and kissed him three times on his forehead. He then lightly punched him in the stomach before body-slamming him onto the couch. Pax rolled himself into a ball, laughing. Ukweli sat on the couch beside him.

"Have you been taking care of your sister?"

"Yes, sir," Pax answered, still laughing.

"Have you been taking care of your mother?"

Pax cleared his throat and stopped laughing. "Yes, sir."

"Have you been taking care of Mrs. Bergstrom?"

"Ahh, no, sir."

"Well, why not?"

"Mrs. Bergstrom takes care of us."

"And your mother doesn't?" Ukweli was confused.

"She's sad a lot. So I take care of her."

"Oh Pax, stop being dramatic." Kiera walked into the room, lifted Pax from the couch, and sat in his place beside Ukweli with Pax in her lap. "He thinks I'm sad anytime I'm not laughing." Kip climbed into Ukweli's lap.

"Daddy, what did you bring me?"

"Oh, I don't know, but if I were you, I would definitely stay away from that big black bag by the door." Both kids hopped up and ran to the big black bag by the door.

Kip and Pax emerged from the back bedroom smelling of bubble bath and powder, fully dressed for bed. They jumped onto the couch, spilling some of the popcorn out of the large bowl that sat between Ukweli and Kiera.

"Can we watch the movie too?"

Kiera feigned regret. "No, you can't. The language isn't sprout friendly."

"Aww, we've heard it all before."

Ukweli stepped in. "Not tonight, Pax. Sorry, buddy."

"Yes, sir."

The children made a solemn walk to the bedroom while Kiera stood up from the couch to see Mrs. Bergstrom to the door.

"Thank you, Mrs. Bergstrom. The kids really had fun today."

"Dear, have you had a chance to speak with your husband?"

"No, I haven't. I don't like to unload on him when he's just coming off a mission."

"He's your husband and he loves you. He'll understand."

"I know. I'll talk to him soon."

Mrs. Bergstrom stepped outside and Kiera closed the door behind her. She got to the couch in time to see Ukweli's entire face submerged in the popcorn bowl.

"UK, why?" He lifted his face from the bowl. A few kernels were stuck to his eyelids.

"It keeps the butter off my hands."

"So, you would rather it be on your face?"

"You can clean it off." He lowered his voice and raised his left brow.

"Uhh, I'm not licking popcorn butter off your face, UK." She stepped into the kitchen.

"You know you want to." Ukweli moved his head side to side.

"Quit being ridiculous." She threw him a hand towel and sat down so their legs touched.

"Your loss. This butter is delicious. Is it garlic butter?"

"No. It's just regular butter."

"Oh, okay. Well, kudos. You make a great popcorn bowl."

"Thanks, I guess."

"Do you have the remote? You ready for naked movie night?" Ukweli started removing his shirt.

"Can I ask you a question first?"

Ukweli pulled his shirt back down. "Oh, of course. What's up?"

"What's going on with you and Mendoza?" Kiera was now sitting with her legs crisscrossed on the couch.

Ukweli leaned to the side. "Kiera, really? This again?"

"UK, I'm not a fool. I love you and I'm willing to work through this. I know I've been preoccupied with the kids, so I'm not even blaming you."

"Blaming me? What is it that you think you know?"

"I know she's in love with you. I've seen the text messages you think you delete. I know you go to see Dr. Eriksson before you come home. I know you do that out of respect for me. I know you love me, but I also know you have feelings for her that maybe you don't understand. But it's there."

"Kiera . . ."

"Look, if you insist on continuing to lie to me, that's fine. We'll have a sham marriage and I'll just keep focusing my energy on the kids while you chase a ghost all over the world and continue giving yourself to your mistress—"

"Wait." Ukweli sat up straight and put his hand on Kiera's knee.

"Wait for wh—"

"Shhh."

"What is it, UK?"

"I think I'm . . . sensing."

"Sensing what?"

"There's a torq here."

"What?"

Ukweli stood up and took a deep breath. He closed his eyes. The hair on his arms and on the back of his neck swayed.

"It's . . . calling me. It's trying to communicate with me. It knows I'm sensing it."

"I thought you didn't do that anymore."

"I haven't, since the Caribbean."

"Where is it? Is it here? In this room?"

"No. It's in the basement. Grab the kids and go to the bedroom."

"UK, are you—"

"Kiera, go. Now." Ukweli went to the kitchen pantry and grabbed a revolver and a dagger and walked toward the basement. He walked slowly and quietly down the stairs. When he reached the bottom, he flipped the light switch. Each of the four lights in the corner of the room powered on and suddenly popped off. The room remained dark except for the Seer logo on the computer screen. Ukweli took small steps away from the stairs when he started to feel immense pressure. The rolling chair at his computer desk slowly turned to face him. It was empty.

"I know you're here."

"Of course you do. I called to you." The sound was like hearing ten ominous whispering voices at once.

"How did you get into my home?"

"I came in with you."

"That's impossible. I would never allow torqueo anima near my family."

"I am eternally higher than torqueo anima."

"I don't care what you claim to be. You are not welcome here."

"Yet you have invited me in." As the demon spoke, it began to materialize. It stood. It was the shape of a man, a very large man, outlined in bright alternating blue-and-red pulsing light. The face continuously changed between demonic forms; a skull, an evil clown, a long-toothed beast, a disfigured man, a dragon, a red warrior.

"A mistake I will correct now." Ukweli swung his dagger at the advancing figure and the consistency of the demon's body was like water. There was resistance on contact, and then his hand and dagger went straight through. The adversary's advance was unaffected.

The demon threw a long, slow punch that Ukweli avoided just before unleashing a barrage of punches into the midsection of its form. Ukweli grabbed the torq by the throat before his hand closed on air. The demon launched a powerful kick to Ukweli's chest, knocking him to the floor.

"Your resistance is useless." The demon stood over Ukweli.

"Tell me why you are here." Ukweli coughed.

"I'm here to help you."

"You're here to help me? With what?"

"I am Yazata. I represent the one true and living god. The god of truth. The god of life. The god of power."

"His name is Thysia. I know him." Ukweli slowly began to stand.

"You are misled. The being you call Thysia is one of many who serve the will of the true god."

"And who is this god?"

"She goes by many names, but you can call her Mithras. She is pleased that you have invited her here."

"I have certainly done no such thing."

"She inhabits your dark passions. She flourishes in your indulgence."

"Dark passions?"

"In her merciful wisdom, she is graciously offering to grow you as a member of her court."

"Then she knows nothing of me."

"She knows you all too well. As you lie with your mistress, she is there. As you take pleasure in death and violence, she is there. She lives in your memories in Lagos Island as you stood, alone, in your sister's blood. She has been pruning you since you were a boy. She is the vine. You are the branch."

"Tell your queen she is not welcome here."

"Your actions have dictated otherwise. That choice is no longer yours to make. She offers you a power greater than any you have ever known. You will rule this planet and beyond. Glory to Mithras!" The figure delivered a blow to Ukweli's face, knocking him to the ground, unconscious. The being then turned into a mist and faded away. There was no hissing. There was a fading sound of trumpets.

When Ukweli regained consciousness twenty minutes later, he was lying on the floor in the basement with his head in Kiera's lap. She was crying and lightly tapping his face. He coughed and took a deep breath and she kissed him.

"What happened, UK?"

"You're right. We need to talk."

JULY 17, 2050

Vasher sat in the Mithraeum in London with his face in his hands. He hadn't heard from Yazata in months, and he was concerned that his streak of narrow escapes was cause for concern. He had become very wealthy since pledging allegiance to Mithras, and he had a natural affinity for creating chaos. In fact, that was the only assignment Yazata had given him so far, causing chaos. The fact that Mithras was curiously mobilizing versus the Seers was icing on the cake.

Vasher's father had been a minister in Makurdi and a professor of religion at Benue State University. Vasher's parents also ran a shelter on the outskirts of the city where they instilled religious principles and provided food, clothing, hygiene products, and job training for the less fortunate, widows, and orphans in the city.

Vasher was sixteen years old when he and his parents watched from Kano as Dr. Kobe Aseyori gave an address from the rose garden at the White House in the United States. They were proud of their fellow Nigerian, but expressed concern over his evolving beliefs. Two weeks later, Vasher's parents died defending their church during the Dark Reveal. Vasher was present and tried to help but was struck on the back of the head with a large wooden torch. He regained consciousness in time to drag his mother from the burning building. He never found his father. His mother, as she rested her head in her son's lap, coughed, opened her eyes to see the church engulfed in flames, let out a gut-wrenching scream, and took her last breath.

Vasher blamed the god of the church for not responding to his desperate pleas when his parents died. After some research and travel, he decided to follow the tenants of Mithraism, pledging his soul to the goddess in exchange for the opportunity to kill Kobe Aseyori. When the Dragon beat him to it, he decided Ukweli's life would be a suitable consolation prize.

That was until he was approached by Yazata with an alternate plan.

He sat alone inside the Mithraeum. The site had become a tourist attraction in the Walbrook area of London and was usually bustling with guests, but the facility was closed on Mondays and only those with special clearance were allowed inside. As Vasher nervously waited, his breathing labored from the anxiety, he was suddenly in the presence of Yazata. Vasher fell to one knee and bowed his head. The layered voice of Yazata startled him.

"The priest and his message remain unchanged."

"Yes. The Seers knew of our plan. They were able to evacuate him."

"Can your goddess count on you? Should we make new arrangements?"

"No. I will get to the priest."

"For your sake. You must ensure that Captain Aseyori continues to track you. As long as your presence is enough to motivate his pursuits . . . keep him occupied and your goddess will spare you."

"I humbly request more resources. The Seers have decimated what remained of Imperium, and each confrontation reduces my meager forces by hundreds."

"Hal tushukik fi hukm alaihati?" Though Yazata spoke calmly, Vasher put his hands on his temples and his ears began to bleed.

"No, never! The goddess has provided at every turn, and I am grateful for her blessings!"

"Good. The captain will return to Zurich from the west soon. Be prepared to mobilize. Every moment he spends home in Zurich . . . jeopardizes the mission."

"I am always ready to serve my goddess." Vasher took a breath and lifted his head. Yazata was gone.

4

DAKOTA AND BRYCE

Dakota Williams was born July 20, 2043, in Atlanta. Though he was three months premature, he was healthy and weighed four pounds at birth. Due to unforeseen and unfortunate circumstances, Dakota was given up for adoption and taken in by Millie Williams, the wife of Parker Williams, a wealthy, Stanford-educated tech tycoon. Unable to conceive herself, Millie raised Dakota with love and care as if he were her biological child.

Millie enrolled Dakota in the Atlanta International School, where he learned Portuguese and began studying Italian, and Parker's connections in the city allowed Dakota to begin soccer training at the Atlanta United Academy.

In the early morning hours of New Year's Day 2050, Parker Williams was snatched from behind the wheel of his luxury SUV, beaten to within an inch of his life, and left bloody and unconscious at the side of the road, his head resting on a piece of discarded gum on the sidewalk.

Citing the lower crime rates, Parker moved his family to Zurich on Dakota's seventh birthday.

Bryce James was born in October of 2042. He wasn't sure when exactly his birthday was. He was found in a dumpster in Atlanta by Penny James in April of 2043, and she guessed he was about six months old.

Penny James was a hooker. She ran away from home when she was sixteen after years of being sexually abused by her mother's live-in boyfriends. She met Big Truck after being on her own for about a year. Big Truck, twenty-eight when he met Penny, took her in as one of his girlfriends. Big Truck was one of the biggest opioid dealers in the South, and he lived with his five girlfriends in an apartment in the Buckhead district of Atlanta. Big Truck pimped his girlfriends out to his business partners in the pharmaceutical space who controlled his supply line. The other four girls didn't like Penny because Big Truck showed her the most attention. She was beautiful, brilliant, and ruthless. It was Penny who suggested that Big Truck start moving his money to a Swiss account. She handled the transactions for him.

When Penny found Bryce in the dumpster, she got Big Truck's permission to keep him, with the caveat that Big Truck would never be responsible for him. Penny raised Bryce on her own. She never enrolled him in school. Instead, she let him watch educational videos on her computer. Bryce learned everything he knew from watching YouTube videos . . . and Penny. He learned how to count using pills and dirty money. He learned to speak English and Spanish by watching Penny interact with the gang members who moved their product on the streets. He loved to cook and learned new recipes online. He learned how to use a gun too.

Once, when Penny and Big Truck were arguing, Bryce stepped in, trying to protect Penny. Big Truck slapped him and he fell to the floor bleeding from his mouth and nose. The next day, Penny got Bryce a birth certificate, establishing his official birthdate as October 11, 2042, and she got passports for the two of them. She swore to Bryce, in the hearing of Big Truck, that he would never be in danger as long as she lived. One year later, Penny and Big Truck got into a heated argument and Big Truck punched Penny and broke her nose. Bryce came to her aid and pointed a gun at Big Truck.

He stood between them and shouted, "Leave my mama alone!"

"What you gone do with that, lil man?" Big Truck took a toothpick out of his mouth.

"Leave my mama alone." Bryce kept both hands on the gun pointed at Big Truck's face.

"Or what? What you gone do?" Big Truck smiled, revealing the four gold teeth that replaced his canines.

"I ain't gone say it again." Bryce pulled back the hammer on the gun until it clicked.

Big Truck started walking toward him. Bryce calmly and confidently pulled the trigger twice, striking Big Truck once in the head and once in the chest. Big Truck fell to the floor dead.

Penny got up and took the gun and grabbed the emergency bag she kept for the two of them. They rode metro transit to the airport and flew to Switzerland. When they arrived, they took a taxi to a house in Zurich. One year earlier, when Penny and Big Truck had gotten into their first fight, Penny had purchased a home and a car in

Zurich. She would now begin a new life with Bryce in a new country, aided by the four million francs she had deposited in Lombard Odier Bank on Big Truck's behalf.

Dakota Williams and Bryce James enrolled in International School—Zurich North, where they met their new friend, Pax Aseyori. The three shared interests in soccer, science, and languages. With their dads frequently out of the country, or out of the picture, the three boys, along with their mothers, became close friends. Kiera, Millie, and Penny bonded over their love of all things merlot and their sons' commonalities.

Kip did not like Bryce, but found herself oddly drawn to Dakota.

(5)

EVERYTHING CHANGED (THE FIRST TIME)

SEPTEMBER 12, 2050

Ukweli, dressed in combat armor with a full weapons set, sat on a desk that once belonged to a third-grade teacher. The Atlanta Public Schools Board of Education had decided to close the facility at the end of the 2049–50 school year due to what some of the teachers described as disturbing paranormal activity. Parents threatened to pull their children from the district and teachers put in for transfers. The district had decided to just redistribute the faculty and student body and close the school permanently. Some of the citizens thought it was a waste of money to let a sound building go vacant because of a series of tall tales. The leader of the Church of the Seer knew better.

Ukweli sat patiently and looked around the room. The walls were still decorated with student work and encouraging

39

posters, and it occurred to him that the classroom Pax sat in every day likely resembled this space in some ways. He closed his eyes, just for a moment, and allowed himself to think of his home in Zurich. It was full of the people who meant the most to him. It was his . . .

Ukweli felt his skin crawl. He opened his eyes and was not surprised to see ten men in the room.

He sipped from a plastic cup containing cold brew. "Gentlemen, it's always nice to be a part of your gatherings."

The torq in the front addressed Ukweli. "Captain, we have no quarrel with you. Why are you here?"

"I'm looking for Vasher."

"We have no affiliation with Vasher or Imperium."

"Torqueo anima with no affiliation with Imperium? Who is your master?"

"We are in the service of the goddess Mithras."

"Why are you here?"

"Because you are here."

Ukweli's eyes grew intense. The men took a step back. "Because I'm here?" He placed his right hand on his chest.

"You came looking for a fight. The goddess Mithras inhabits your dark passions."

"I'm trying to end the war with Imperium. Why does your goddess consider that a dark passion?"

"You're here to take life. The stresses of your existence have continuously driven you to violence. The very thing that makes you formidable also serves as a beacon for Mithras. That is why she has chosen you. Your natural inclinations summon the goddess."

"As I told your boss, I have no interest in serving Mithras."

"Your taste for violence suggests otherwise."

"Well, I certainly didn't come downtown for nothing."

Ukweli drew his sword and the men advanced. As Ukweli prepared to engage, he felt a sharp pain in his chest that bent him to a knee. The pain was like fire and radiated from his chest and stomach out to his arms. The torqs halted, unsure as to what was happening in front of them. After another few seconds, Ukweli stood, his eyes black like coal. The torqs moved quickly to attack only to have Ukweli move side to side with supernatural speed and aggression. Ukweli was aware of his power as the torqs seemed to move in slow motion. He slashed and stabbed his way through the group of machines until the last of them fell and the demons hissed and dissolved. The brown of Ukweli's eyes returned and his heart rate slowed. His breathing continued in a labored fashion as he fought to understand what had just occurred. He had never felt so powerful and so out of control. It was as if he were a torq himself.

"The darkness is present. The harvest will be grand."

"The darkness cannot be harvested until it is mature. Continue to apply pressure."

"He grows more powerful with each emergence. I fear if we wait too long, he may be too powerful to overcome."

"He will never have the power of our combined strength. We will subdue him. The plan is flawless. Stay the course."

Ukweli walked into the Church of the Seer headquarters in downtown Atlanta. It was a thing he had done hundreds of times before, but it had been a while and this time felt different. He entered the decontamination chamber and was coated in a dehydrated alcohol powder designed to neutralize any pathogens that might exist in torq blood. The process was familiar and gave him a sense of peace. He entered the locker room and removed his armor and prepared to head for the showers. A soft voice came over the speaker.

"Captain."

"Hey."

"Did you find any answers?"

"I guess. Not what I wanted, though."

"You drew your weapon?"

"Yes."

"Was there gore?"

"Yes. The cleanup unit was already on site when I left, though. No worries."

"So, you're okay?"

"Yeah, I'm headed to the showers."

"You need help?"

"You might want to sit this one out. I'm pretty grimy."

"Nonsense."

Mendoza took the elevator to the first floor and quickly navigated the staircase to the lockers. She entered the level with a spritely gait and struggled to contain her excitement as she meandered to the third stall and found Ukweli soaking himself under the flood from the large waterfall showerhead. She tried to stay calm, but she loved this man, and it made her heart cartwheel to see him standing there, close enough to touch. She undressed, stepped into the shower, hugged him from behind, and let the same water wash her cares away.

After a few minutes, when she could convince her arms to let go, she grabbed the soap and began to wash his back.

Ukweli didn't respond to her presence. He just continued to stand under the water.

"You're very quiet. Is everything okay?" Ukweli didn't respond. "Hey, I'm serious. What's going on?" Still nothing. "So, you're just not gonna talk to me at all?" Ukweli continued to stand still under the heavy shower flow. "Fine. I'll leave you to it."

"Wait." Ukweli turned and gently grabbed her arm. She snatched it away.

"What?" Mendoza rolled her eyes.

"We need to talk."

"I've been trying to talk to you."

"I know. I'm sorry. Get dressed. I'll meet you in the office."

"Get dressed? Dang, something really is wrong, huh?" Mendoza smirked and stepped out of the shower. Ukweli sighed and stepped back under the cascading water.

Ukweli stepped off the elevator and took the short walk to the central office. Mendoza was seated in the side chair at the conference table closest to the master chair where Ukweli generally sat. She wore a pink sweatsuit and had her head down on the table with the hood over her hair when Ukweli walked in. She held her head up and Ukweli could see the worry in her face. He sat down.

"Hey."

"Hey."

"Claire, we've been through enough together. This doesn't have to be awkward."

"We'll see about that." Mendoza sat up with her elbows on the table and clasped her hands.

"Okay, do you want to go first?"

"No, you should definitely go first."

"Claire, we have to stop seeing each other." Ukweli looked up into Mendoza's eyes as if he were a cat staring at fish swimming in a bowl.

"What?!"

"Look, I know we have strong feelings for each other—"

"Feelings? I'm in love with you. I left my life for you."

"Claire, you know I love my wife. You know I love my children."

"Okay, maybe I should've gone first."

"Why? What is it?"

"Rahisi . . . I'm pregnant."

"What? How?"

"What do you mean how?"

"Do you know who—"

"Yes. You."

"Are you sure? What about . . ."

"I've told you, too many times, that I don't sleep with PT. He's fun, but that's it. Plus, I think he might be gay."

"Yeah, well, he named himself PonyTail. In retrospect, that should've been a red flag."

"UK . . ."

"How far along are you?"

"Almost three months. It must've happened in Miami."

"Kiera is gonna kill me."

"You'll have to tell her about us."

"She knows about us."

"What?"

"She confronted me back in the summer. She's known for a while."

"When were you gonna tell me?"

"Now. That's what I wanted to talk about . . . among other things."

"Other things?"

"Have you ever heard of the goddess Mithras?"

"No."

"Well, I'll have to explain it to you later. Just know that things between you and I have gotten pretty complicated."

"More complicated than the fetus currently planted in my uterus?"

"Touché."

"Look, if she already knows about us, maybe we can sit down, the three of us, and just have a conversation."

"Of course. Hey, Kiera, you know my mistress that I've been sleeping with and lying to you about and that you've grown to hate? Well, she's carrying my child. And, oh yeah, she's in love with me. Cool?"

"Don't say that."

Ukweli tried to smile, but he was beginning to feel the weight of his decisions. *How could I have allowed things to get this far off track? Maybe the team was right.*

Mendoza tried to hold an encouraging tone. "Hey, listen to me. I love you. And despite what you have to tell the world, you love me too. I know this complicates things. But we'll get through it. We'll make the necessary adjustments and we'll do right by our child."

"It'll be the guillotine for me for sure."

"Hey, it's not my fault if she can't control her man." Ukweli raised an eyebrow. "I'm just kidding! I know how important she is to you. Listen, we can do this. Better yet, we have to do this."

What on earth have I done?

Coach Hassan stood on the edge of the practice field and looked over the young players moving through drills with his assistant coaches. He had the most talented youth squad in Switzerland and he was excited to hear that Ukweli Aseyori's kid was looking for new training grounds. Coach Hassan had faced off against Ukweli's Tottenham squad in UEFA matches as a member of Zurich FC and in Confederation of African Football matches as a member of the Egyptian national team. The Super Eagles and the Pharaohs had developed a budding rivalry after the teams faced off in a 2042 World Cup knockout match decided by penalty kicks.

As Coach Hassan watched as his players moved fluidly through individual drills, Millie Parker approached him to make an introduction.

"Excuse me, Coach Hassan." He turned to face her with his whistle in his mouth. "I would like you to meet Kiera Aseyori." He released his whistle and extended his hand.

"Mrs. Aseyori, pleased to meet you."

"Coach Hassan, the pleasure is mine. You have developed quite a program here."

"Please, call me Brad. And I'm just a figurehead. The real stars are my assistant coaches and, of course, my very talented players."

"Ahh, a futile attempt at humility." Kiera realized they were still shaking hands and gently let go.

Coach Hassan raised his left brow. "Am I really that transparent?" They both smiled.

Kiera found it impossible to ignore the contrast of Coach Hassan's dazzling white teeth against the backdrop of his olive skin. She recognized him to be a beautiful man.

"This is my son, Pax." Pax stood beside his mother and looked on with apprehension.

Coach Hassan knelt in front of Pax and looked him in the eyes. "Hello, Pax. I hear you're a very talented player."

"Yes, sir."

"You know, I played against your dad back in the day. Did he tell you?"

"He told me he always beat you."

"Ah, I see. Are you as good as your dad?"

Pax didn't flinch. "I'm better."

Coach Hassan stood and looked at Kiera. "Yes, I do believe he'll fit in just fine."

Dakota and Bryce noticed Pax and ran over to greet him. Pax hugged his mom and left with the boys to join the drills.

Kiera cleared her throat. "I do apologize for his cockiness. We raised him to be confident, but sometimes he can take it a little too far."

"Oh, please. No apology necessary. I remember what Ukweli was like as a player. You know what they say about the apple and the tree."

"I guess."

"Did Ukweli really tell Pax that he always beat me?"

"That is assuredly true." They smiled again. Kiera pulled her hair behind her right ear.

"Well, let me get this practice started. I hope to see you again soon." He blew his whistle and jogged onto the field without waiting for a response.

Millie slid a few steps closer to Kiera, her expression dripping with pettiness. "Well, someone has a new fan."

Kiera looked confused. "What are you talking about, Millie?"

"Oh please, woman. Coach Hassan is the best-looking man in this city and every soccer mom has been trying to get his attention. But I haven't seen him look at anyone the way he just looked at you."

Kiera scoffed at Millie's antics. "You're so dramatic."

"I am and I know it, but not about this. That man is into you."

"Millie, please."

"Listen, Ukweli and Parker are off traveling the world, fighting wars and boards of directors and such. What's wrong with us enjoying the view?"

"Millie, if I didn't know better, I would think you have inappropriate plans for Brad."

"Let me tell you something, if he ever looked at me the way he just looked at you? Giiirrrlll."

"You're silly."

By then, Penny had joined the group and added her insight. "And he's never told any of us to call him Brad."

Millie raised and lowered her shoulders with her palms facing upward.

NOVEMBER 23, 2050

Ukweli walked through the front door as quietly as he could. He didn't want to disturb the sprouts if they were taking their afternoon nap. Honestly, he hoped Kiera was asleep too. There was a conversation looming that he had been dreading for months. It was time to talk, though, and it couldn't wait. He wished it could wait.

He sat the big black bag by the door and tiptoed through the entryway into the kitchen where he found Mrs. Bergstrom making peanut butter crackers. She looked up and smiled. Ukweli smiled back. He was glad to see her.

"Mrs. Bergstrom." Ukweli raised his hand to his forehead and lowered his face as if tipping his cap.

"Good afternoon, Captain. Welcome home." She sat the

spoon on the tray and walked around the island to hug him. He kissed her on the cheek.

"Thank you. It's good to see you."

"How was New Zealand?" Mrs. Bergstrom walked while she listened and grabbed the spoon to continue her culinary duties.

"It's a beautiful country."

"Were you and your team able to apprehend your suspect?"

"No, ma'am. Somehow, he continues to elude us."

"Oh well. I'm sure you'll get him next time." She spoke with her face down as she chopped celery stalks.

"If only I could be so sure. Where are the sprouts?"

"They're taking a nap. I'm making them a snack for afterward. Would you like me to get them?"

"No, no, please. Thanks. I need to talk to Kiera, and it's probably better if they're asleep."

"Would you like me to take them out for snacks instead? So you and the lady can have some privacy?"

"Let's keep that on the table, just in case."

Kiera walked into the kitchen from a back room. She was excited to see Ukweli and started to approach him when she noticed the serious look on his face. She continued to walk toward him, but she walked slowly.

"Hey, babe. Everything okay?"

"Hello, beautiful. I'm fine, but no, everything is not okay."

Kiera kept walking until she was close enough to embrace Ukweli. She hugged him and placed her hands just behind his ears. She kissed him. "Do you want to talk about it?"

Ukweli looked at the floor. "Yeah, we need to talk. Go ahead and sit in the living room. I'll be right back." He turned and walked out the front door.

Mrs. Bergstrom poured two small cups of milk and placed them on a tray beside the plates. She lifted the tray from the countertop and started to walk toward the back of the house. "Kiera, dear, it'll be fine. He's your husband and he loves you."

"Yeah, I know . . . I think." Kiera sat on the couch and Mrs. Bergstrom disappeared down the hall and into the playroom.

After four minutes, Ukweli came back into the house, rolling a metallic pink suitcase as he walked behind Mendoza. Kiera glanced at Mendoza long enough to realize there was a small bulge showing through the midsection of her jacket. Kiera stared through Ukweli. She watched as he gently escorted Mendoza to the black leather recliner and helped her into the seat, even though she didn't need help. He walked to the couch and sat beside Kiera without ever looking at her. They were close enough for their knees to touch, but she slid over a few inches so they wouldn't.

Ukweli took a deep breath and looked up for the first time. "Kiera . . ." He paused. Kiera just kept looking at him. "So, we need to talk."

"I'm sitting right in front of you, UK. Talk. I'm all ears."

"Right. Okay." Ukweli rubbed his pants like they were dirty or on fire.

"And you can skip the part where you tell me she's pregnant. That's obvious. And she wouldn't be here if it wasn't yours. So, you can skip that part too."

"Okay . . . so where do you want me to start?"

"You can start with an apology." Kiera was surprisingly calm, and it put Ukweli on edge. He fully expected her to melt down, and the fact that she sat upright and spoke directly to him while looking him in the face was giving him a flood of anxiety. This was more intense than combat, and he wasn't sure what to do or say.

"An apology?"

"Yes. Let's see, you could try, Kiera, I'm sorry for putting the missions ahead of my family. Kiera, I'm sorry for being gone for long periods of time away from you and the children. Kiera, I'm sorry that when I had no time for you and the sprouts, I somehow made time for Men-DOH-za. Kiera, I'm sorry for lying to you. Kiera, I'm sorry for breaking your trust. Kiera, I'm sorry for further complicating our already dysfunctional family. Feel free to start with any of those."

"Kiera, I'm sorry."

"Oh, shut up."

"But you said—"

"How far along is she?"

"Uhh . . ." Ukweli felt like his brain was on fire. He simply couldn't think of an appropriate response. The truth suddenly seemed totally inappropriate.

Kiera rolled her eyes and turned her attention, and her gaze, to the recliner. Mendoza wore light-colored jeans with pink-and-white sneakers and a white shirt under her pink letter jacket. There was a white block *C* on the left side of her jacket. Her skin was slightly fairer than usual, and her black hair stopped obediently at her shoulders. Her makeup and fingernails were flawless, particularly surprising for someone who had just come from the airport. *She probably got a manicure on the jet.* The thought made Kiera furious. Mendoza sat quietly as she sipped from a large purple cup of warm water with a sprig of mint and a slice of lime.

"Good afternoon, Mendoza."

"Hi, Kiera." Mendoza waved and quickly returned her mouth to her straw.

"Was your flight comfortable?" The sarcasm dripped like melting ice.

"Ten hours of bliss."

"How far along are you?"

"Five months." Mendoza held up her left hand with her fingers extended.

"Five months?"

"Yes."

Kiera softly placed her right hand over her heart as if she were saying the pledge of allegiance. "And you're in my house right now because my husband is the father?"

"Yes."

Kiera took a deep breath. "Do you love him?"

Ukweli interrupted, "Now wait, Kiera—"

Kiera calmly but sharply turned to Ukweli. "Shut up, Ukweli. I'm talking to Mendoza now." She returned her attention to the big chair. "Mendoza, do you love him?"

"Yes."

Kiera sighed and stood up. She held her hand to her forehead. "I need a cigarette."

Ukweli chuckled. "You don't smoke."

"Don't tell me what I don't do and don't pretend to know me." Kiera began to pace the floor.

"I'm not. I'm sorry. Just sit down and let me tell you my plan."

"Ukweli, if you're about to tell me you're leaving me for Mendoza . . ."

"I'm not."

"Because you didn't have to bring her here for that."

"I didn't."

"If you're telling me you're moving this bitch into my house . . ."

"Settle down. I'm not."

"Then please tell me why the hell she's here. She *got* pregnant in Atlanta. Why can't she just *be* pregnant in Atlanta?"

Mendoza cleared her throat and raised her hand. "I got pregnant in Miami."

Kiera whirled to face her. Ukweli put his hand out. "Claire, you're not helping."

"Ohhh, *KUH-LAY-ER*, is it? Well, let me tell you something, Claire—"

Ukweli stood up, prepared to restrain his wife. "Kiera, please. Just let me tell you my plan before you say something you might regret."

Kiera stepped away and looked him up and down. "I can promise you, I won't regret *anything* I say to you or your knocked-up side bitch."

Mendoza rolled her eyes. "Well, that was mean."

"Again, Claire, not helping."

"I need some air." Kiera stormed off through the kitchen and out the front door.

"See, I think that went swimmingly." Mendoza slurped the last bit of water from the bottom of her cup.

Outside, Kiera walked to the edge of the driveway with one foot on the narrow, gravel, one-way road that gave the house access to the town. She wore black yoga pants with a form-fitting black top, and royal-blue cross-trainers. Wearing her hair in a bun allowed the sun to add a glow to her perfect skin. As she stood, looking through the backyard at the river, she began to cry. All she had ever really wanted was to be a great mother. Now that her husband had betrayed her trust, she wondered if she would ever have the family she always dreamed of. She blamed Ukweli for what he had done to her while, all along, blaming herself for allowing it. She was confused, embarrassed, angry, disappointed, and hurt. Just then, Coach Hassan pulled his car over on the road and stopped in front of her.

"Hello there. Is everything okay?" He was leaning toward the passenger window.

"Oh, hi, Brad. Yes, I'm fine. Thank you."

"Are you sure? Those don't look like happy tears."

"I was just . . . watching a sad movie." She softly wiped her tears with her hands.

"I'm on my way into town for ice cream. I would be honored to share your company."

"I don't think so. Thank you, though."

"They say there's magical healing powers in waffle cones. You sure?"

Kiera smiled. "That's very nice of you, but I'll have to pass."

"Oh, come on. It's right around the corner. I'll have you there and back before anyone even knows you're gone." Kiera started to speak but paused. "Please don't make me eat ice cream alone. People will start to think I'm crazy."

She smiled again. "How do I know you're *not* crazy?"

Coach Hassan flashed a smile that made her shiver. She hadn't noticed another man in quite a while, and it made her feel guilty, like she had committed a minor crime. He softly patted the passenger seat. "I guess you'll just have to trust me." Kiera turned and looked at the house for a moment. Then she got in the car.

Twelve minutes later, they returned to the house and Kiera was not surprised to see Ukweli sitting on the front steps. His forearms rested on his thighs just above his knees and he held a black pistol with a silencer in his right hand and a tightly wrapped Cuban cigar in his left hand. Kiera, sensing the rising testosterone in the atmosphere, decided to head the situation off at the pass.

"Hey, thanks for the ice cream. I'm gonna head inside." She opened her door.

Coach Hassan opened his door. "You need me to walk you to the porch?"

Kiera raised an eyebrow and chuckled. "Do you have a death wish?"

He closed his door. "Are you serious? Is he serious? With the gun and all?"

She snickered. "He is."

"Then maybe I *should* walk you to the door?"

"Brad, that pistol isn't for me. I'll be fine. Thanks for the treat."

Kiera got out of the car, calmly shut the door, and stood on the street to watch Coach Hassan drive away. When he was safely out of sight, she turned and walked to the house. She stood in front of Ukweli and took a long, deliberately provocative lick of her ice cream cone. Ukweli wasn't impressed.

"You think you're funny?"

"Why? Because I like ice cream?" She licked the ice cream again.

Ukweli stood. "You called this fool to my house?"

"Is Mendoza still in *my* house?" Ukweli was silent. Kiera stepped around him and climbed the stairs to the front porch. When she reached the top she turned. "Oh, and put that thing away. Loaded firearms aren't safe to have around the unborn."

PAX

When I think about a
Fight night, midnight flight
Benz in black, Jag in white
Drop top, hit the block
Car slows down but the rims don't stop
Ice in my chains, Ice on my wrist
Anything she wants, just add it to the list
Fresh new Js, Air Force Ones
Don't worry 'bout the money, baby, I got tons
'Cause when I take my lady on a shopping spree
She chill on the check 'cause it's all on me
But if she can't decide what she wanna do first
While we're riding up the coast . . . I flip a coin
I flip a coin, I flip a coin
I flip a coin 'cause it's already done

They already know when I walk in the joint
She ain't gotta say a word, all she does is point
Get it off the shelf, take it off the rack

She made a special order, go get it from the back
Because she knows that if she wants it and they got it
Then they can bag it and there ain't a doubt about it
My baby knows that I am willing and able
And she ain't gotta swipe a card, I throw a stack on the table
I keep that girl in so much ice it might make my baby shiver
Because this money flowing in like it's the Euphrates River
The yacht is parked in Monaco, the jet will land in Dubai
When shawty friends be peeping all they say is girl you too fly
He got you in a gated house, your car got suicide doors
What a girl like me gotta do to get a man like yours
I flip a coin, I flip a coin
Heads or Tails, Either way, She knows she already won
—Lyrics from the hit song "Flip a Coin"
By JetPack (featuring PonyTail)

DECEMBER 3, 2050

Mendoza had now been living in the family home in Zurich for ten days. The apartment Ukweli prepared for her had a suspicious plumbing disaster that had caused flooding and set the construction crew back three weeks. Ukweli didn't trust the security at the local hotels, so she had been staying in the extra bedroom.

It was very common for Ukweli and Kiera to perform for the sprouts during breakfast. Sometimes Ukweli would rap and Kiera would dance with Pax. Kiera would often sing while Ukweli danced with Kip. Their mornings were always lively and active. Over the course of the past ten days, however, Ukweli and Kiera rarely spoke to each other. They didn't eat breakfast together. They didn't even eat breakfast with the sprouts. Mrs. Bergstrom served breakfast for the children while their parents mostly avoided each other. They didn't argue, but the silence was deafening.

Pax rarely saw Mendoza. She did a good job of staying hidden. He knew she was the problem, though. His parents always expressed love for each other in front of them, and Mendoza was the only different thing. He didn't know what she had done, but he knew it was her fault.

Growing increasingly uncomfortable with the tension in the house, Pax spent more and more time in his room alone. He would put on his headphones for physics lectures, language lessons, and, from time to time, music. Pax was a big fan of Atlanta-based rapper JetPack, and his new hit "Flip a Coin" was the one song in the rotation between his educational sessions. Inspired by the lyrics, he would often listen to the song while holding his nineteenth-century Morgan silver dollar, a gift from Mrs. Bergstrom from her late husband's collection. Pax was able to develop a rhythm as he handled his valuable relic that mimicked the deep bass tones coming through his headphones.

On this particular morning, Pax sat at his desk and prepared his computer to stream a physics lecture from Palo Alto. His headphones rested on his neck. For the first time in his life, he heard his parents, their muffled voices pressing against the door, having an argument in the hallway.

"I don't care, UK. Do whatever you want!"

"Why are you so angry now? You know I'm doing everything I can to remedy this."

"I'm sick of looking like a fool!"

"A fool? Love, seriously, where is this coming from?"

"You brought her here because you knew I would just go along with it. You knew I would fall in line like a good soldier. Well, I'm tired of you running over me."

"Kiera, babe, you know that's not my intention."

"Most of the evil in this world is done by people with good intentions."

"Eliot. That's low, Kiera. Using my favorite author against me?"

"If the shoe fits." Kiera took off one of her shoes and threw it at Ukweli. It hit Pax's door on its way to the floor.

"What do you want me to do?!"

"Get her out of my house! Every minute she's here is a new level of disrespect." Kiera stormed off toward the kitchen with footsteps much too heavy for someone her size.

Pax put his hands to his ears and started to cry. Perhaps out of muscle memory, or cosmic alignment, he reached for his favorite coin and gave it a simple flip. As the coin reached the pinnacle of its arc, Pax experienced a distortion in his reality. It was similar to vertigo, only his surroundings shifted side to side instead of in dizzying ellipses. The coin slowly fell into Pax's hand.

"If the shoe fits." A shoe hit Pax's door.

"What do you want me to do?!"

"Get her out of my house! Every minute she's here is a new level of disrespect." He heard his mom's unusually heavy footsteps.

"Kiera, you know I can't control security at the hotels. Her apartment will be ready soon."

"I can't take another week of this!"

Pax looked down at the coin resting in his palm. His green eyes were wide open, shimmering like emeralds. He flipped the coin again. The brief distortion. His mom's footsteps.

"Kiera, you know I can't control security at the hotels. Her apartment will be ready soon."

"I can't take another week of this!"

"It might not be a whole week. Please, just try to be patient. They're working as quickly as they can."

"Maybe I should spend the December holiday season in Egypt!"

Pax grabbed his coin and carefully placed it in his pocket. He was known for studying in his workout gear just in case the urge to train grasped him. He grabbed a soccer ball from the bag in the corner of the room and headed to the backyard for drills. His excitement concerning the obvious tear in the space-time continuum overshadowed his growing concerns over his parents and their tenuous marriage.

(7)

EVERYTHING CHANGED (THE SECOND TIME)

DECEMBER 25, 2050

The December Yuletide celebration found Mendoza, still occupying the hallway bedroom at the Aseyori residence, in the basement lab working the comms. There hadn't been much activity to report, but she had grown weary of playing hide-and-seek with Kiera, and the work of the Church provided a deviation from the status quo. Mendoza missed Ukweli, and though she hated to admit it, she missed PonyTail too. For everything Zurich had to offer, it lacked the pizzazz of Atlanta, and Mendoza was beginning to succumb to the sweats of cabin fever. She was now twenty-five weeks pregnant. She had only gained ten pounds, but she felt like a honey-crusted holiday ham. Everything was swollen, including her face, and she longed for the days when she could go club-hopping or out for dinner and drinks with her friends. Instead, her Yuletide celebration would consist of a green smoothie with kale, Swiss chard, and peppermint and three large computer screens as the algorithms worked to locate Vasher.

Her life wasn't what she thought it would be. When Ukweli demanded she move to Switzerland, she had allowed herself to believe that somewhere, in some faraway galaxy, was a star that would twinkle and grant her the wish for which she so desperately longed. Somehow, she genuinely believed that Ukweli would choose her. She believed he had spared her life in Mongolia because some part of him already loved her. She believed Capricorns and Virgos are compatible such that their bond has great astrological potential. She believed her fortune-teller in Atlanta when she said Mendoza would win the heart of her true love and serve her cosmic purpose. She knew Ukweli cared for her and she believed he loved her, but perhaps not as much as she loved him. Then there was Kiera. Mendoza decided the best way to keep Ukweli's attention, now that her physical body couldn't hold serve, was to show dedication to her job. She figured if she could help Ukweli catch Vasher, he would love her forever.

She sat in front of the screens with her earbuds in, listening to classical music. She hadn't been a fan of the genre until she watched Ukweli train to Bach and had her musical eyes opened to the drama and power of the scales. She loved to listen to the great composers while she worked. It added a sense of strength and accomplishment. She knew she would find Vasher.

As she stared at the moving green, red, and blue lines on the middle monitor, she noticed the basement light came on at the stairs. She heard the footsteps and watched as Ukweli walked down toward her, carrying a single present, crudely wrapped in shiny pink paper. There was a silver ribbon but no bow.

"Mendoza, I'm glad you're up. I hope you were able to rest."

"Ah, the consummate professional. In that case, good morning, Captain."

"Merry Yuletide morning."

"To you and yours as well, sir. How are things upstairs?"

"The sprouts had quite a haul. They seemed pleased."

"And you?"

"I'm pleased that they're pleased."

"No, UK, I'm asking if you got what you wanted."

"My family is happy. That makes me happy."

As Ukweli approached the basement lab, Mendoza stood and they hugged. She quickly returned to her seat. Ukweli cleared his throat.

"This is for you. It's . . . from the sprouts."

"Is that right?" Mendoza looked surprised as she accepted the gift.

Ukweli scratched his head. "Yeah, Pax thought you would like it."

Mendoza slowly opened the present, peeling away the paper and tape. She lifted the lid from the cardboard box inside to reveal two shirts. Both were royal blue, Pax's team colors. The medium shirt had a pink, bejeweled number fifteen on the back with the words "Auntie Claire" above the number. The tiny shirt had the word "Cuz" in pink.

"This is adorable."

"Yeah, I thought so too."

"So, your children believe I'm their long-lost Aunt Claire?"

"It was simpler than the truth."

"Whatever helps you sleep at night, I guess."

"Why do I sense sarcasm?"

"Because you've had me held up here all this time. My apartment was supposed to be ready weeks ago."

"Your apartment is ready now."

"But . . ."

"But what, Claire?"

"But I can't go."

"No."

"Can you tell me why you're paying rent for an apartment that you refuse to let me live in?"

"You're safer here."

"So why the games?"

"Kiera needs to believe I'm making plans for you to leave."

"But you're not."

"No."

"At least tell me this. How much longer will I have to be a pawn in your little game?"

"You're not a pawn and there is no game."

"Then what is going on?"

"The little girl you're carrying means everything to me."

"And what about me, UK? What do I mean to you?"

"You're here, aren't you?"

Mendoza threw her hands in the air and sighed in frustration. As she turned her chair to face the screens, there was a buzz and a call icon appeared.

"This is Kelley calling. You want me to patch it through to your phone?"

"Just put it on the screen."

Mendoza pressed a series of buttons and the video call appeared on the screen. The call was from Kelley's phone, but it wasn't Kelley.

"Hello, Mendoza. Is your boss available?"

Ukweli nudged Mendoza's chair to the side and looked into the camera. "Vasher."

"Merry Yuletide morning, Captain."

"Where is Kelley?"

"Well, that's rude. You can't even return a pleasant greeting?"

"Dammit, Vasher. Where is Kelley?"

"We'll get to that momentarily. How are things going with your . . . family expansion? Has your darling wife finally made her way to greener pastures?"

"Never speak of my family. Where is Kelley?" Ukweli struggled to hide his anger and his growing concern for Kelley.

"Kiera Michaels is one of the most beautiful women in the world. She will certainly be at the top of every eligible bachelor's list once you're dead."

"Her name is Kiera Aseyori. Where is Kelley?"

"She's here." Vasher panned his camera to show Kelley, secured to a chair with duct tape over her legs, torso, and mouth. He grabbed her by her hair and lifted her face so Ukweli could see she was badly beaten.

"No!" Ukweli shouted at the screen. Vasher turned the camera so Alexander was now visible. He was secured to a different chair, though he was not beaten and his mouth wasn't covered. Vasher stood beside Alexander and asked, "Do you have anything to say to your wife before she joins the ancestors?"

Ukweli grabbed the screen. "Vasher, don't do this!"

Vasher peered into the screen. "And why not, Captain? You and your team have been hunting me all over the world. What exactly would you have done to me had you been competent enough to apprehend me? Torture, perhaps?

Death? Most assuredly. Don't think for one moment that I have a sliver of empathy for you or any member of your team."

"This is not the way. We are men of principle! Don't do this!"

By this time, Kiera had made her way down the stairs into the basement. Mendoza was now standing and summoned Kiera to her side, away from the camera. Kiera didn't recognize Vasher, but the agony on Ukweli's face told her everything she needed to know.

Vasher, once again, held the camera to Alexander's face. "Speak from the heart. You won't get a do-over."

Alexander was breathing heavily as he spoke to his wife.

"Kelley, sweetie, can you hear me?" Kelley slowly lifted her head and opened her eyes. "Kelley, you have saved my life one thousand times. When I had questions at every turn, you were the answer to them all. You are my heartbeat. You are my passion. You are my safe haven. My heart safely trusts in you. Many daughters have done virtuously, but you excel them all."

"Touching. Time's up."

There was, suddenly, a single gunshot. Kelley was gone. The video feed ended.

Ukweli released a scream that contained pain, regret, and confusion. It was a scream of focus.

Kiera and Mendoza hugged each other as they cried. Neither approached Ukweli immediately. It dawned on Kiera that Ava would likely have known exactly what to do or say in this moment. Mendoza released Kiera and took a step back. Kiera looked at Mendoza, who gestured for Kiera to go to him. As Kiera approached Ukweli, he fell to his knees. She stood in front of him and he hugged her around her waist and buried his face in her abdomen. He cried for the decisions he had made. He cried for the distractions he had allowed. He cried for the pain he felt. He cried for Alexander's grief and trauma. Mostly, he cried for the loss of his friend and mentor.

After two minutes, Ukweli began to mumble under his breath. "I don't understand. I . . . I just . . . I just don't understand."

Kiera lifted his face with her palms on his ears. "What is it, babe?"

"I just don't understand."

"You don't understand what, UK?"

"Thysia. He . . . he didn't stop it."

Kiera tried to console Ukweli with reason. "UK, you know, these things don't always make sense."

"Thysia allowed Alexander to watch Incursus die in his arms. And now he has watched his wife murdered in front of his eyes. Has Thysia abandoned us? Is this because of me? Have I brought condemnation on my entire community?"

"Of course not, babe. You can't think like that."

"What other way is there to think? Alexander is a good man. His faith in Thysia is stronger than anyone I know. If Thysia will not intervene to prevent this manner of suffering, he has certainly left us all alone." Ukweli hesitated for a few moments. He wiped his face and rose to his feet. He turned to Mendoza. "Call my team, please. Have them meet me at the warehouse in Venice in twelve hours."

"Yes, sir. What should I tell them about Kelley?"

Paul and Kei woke up on Yuletide morning and enjoyed a small breakfast of tamago kake gohan and green tea before heading into town to be with family. They would enjoy games and music in a festive environment before retreating to a more secluded area to exchange small gifts with relatives. The gifts were mostly for the children, but Paul and Kei would also give gifts to each other. They enjoyed the Yuletide celebration into the afternoon.

They left the family gathering to head to the gym for one of their favorite traditions. Paul and Kei often trained together, but very rarely in a versus format. The exception was Yuletide afternoon. This was the one training session that was exclusively competitive combat between the two of them. There was no referee, and the only rule was strict adherence to the safe word.

Paul stood in the corner of the ring wrapping his hands in flexible materials designed to protect the small bones. He always included a plush fabric under his wrap when he fought Kei. She was the most beautiful woman in the world to him, and he had no intention of doing any damage to her face. Aside from her face, abdomen, and kidneys, though, Paul didn't hold punches when he fought Kei. He had learned early in their relationship not to underestimate her abilities—or her competitiveness. She had once broken his jaw and choked him until he passed out with the claim that she never heard the safe word. Their Yuletide combat was brutal and passionate and beautiful.

Kei sat in a chair outside the ring lacing her boots when the communicator in her bag pinged.

Paul looked up. "Was that your Seer's comm?"

Kei grabbed her bag and unzipped the inner pocket. "Yeah. Where is your bag?"

There was a ping from the comm in Paul's bag. "There."

Paul stopped wrapping his hands and climbed out of the ring to walk around to the chair where his bag was sitting.

As he reached into his bag, he heard Kei from across the room.

"It's code Elmo."

"What?" Paul quickly looked up, unable to conceal his shock and concern.

"Let's go into the office." Kei started to gather her items.

"No. There's no one here. Just open it now. What does it say?"

Kei pressed a series of buttons on her communicator and stared at the screen for ten seconds. She suddenly put her hand to her mouth and started crying.

"Kei, what is it?" She didn't respond. Paul opened his device and pressed the key sequence to open the message.

Code: Elmo
From: 010
To: Seer Elite

Black 312

Green 379

45.4408°N, 12.3155°E

21:00

"It . . . it can't be. Kelley?" Kei's voice quivered as she spoke through her disbelief. She sat on the floor with her knees pulled tightly to her chest. Paul quickly grabbed his bag, walked to Kei, and sat behind her. He held her close and rocked her as she cried.

DECEMBER 26, 2050

Ukweli sat in a metal folding chair in the warehouse in

Venice and stared at the lifeless body of Kelley Jack. He had managed to track the location of Kelley's body when Vasher called from her phone. When he found her, she was still taped to a chair, her head slumped over. The blood had stopped dripping and had now begun to dry on her cheeks and arms. He lifted her head and looked into her face, allowing some part of him to hope she would cough or take a breath so he could leap into action and use the emergency medical kit sitting on the floor beside him. He waited for a few minutes, admiring her features, before he let her head fall back into place.

Ukweli recalled his first time in the field with Kelley. She was the Seer who had trained him. She was the only Seer he had ever feared. She was the Seer he admired most. Given her ruthless nature, Ukweli had always expected Kelley to die in the field, yet she had seemed regal, almost godlike, such that he expected her to live forever. Kelley's relationship with Alexander had changed that though. He had seen a previously unknown vulnerability in her, and Alexander had the master key. Perhaps the only key. It made Ukweli sad to know Kelley and Alexander would only be reunited in Caelum.

Ukweli retrieved the dagger from the pocket near his calf and removed the tape from Kelley's legs and forearms. He was careful to kneel in front of her so that when he cut the tape that held her torso to the chair, her body slumped forward into a final embrace. Ukweli lifted her body onto a large metal table and removed her clothes. He grabbed a small bucket, filled it with warm water, and began to sponge her face and neck. Once he was able to get her face clear enough to present to the team, he began to wrap her in linen. He tucked her arms close to her waist and was very careful to respect her privacy. When he had her fully wrapped, he cut enough of the material away from her face so the team could see her. Once he was satisfied with the presentation of her body, he put the materials away, got on his knees beside the table, and allowed himself to embrace the grief.

As his team members arrived at the warehouse, Ukweli welcomed them and gave each of them alone time with Kelley. Once everyone had an opportunity to mourn, they gathered to talk about next steps.

"It's good to see everyone. I'm sorry we haven't gotten together before now. You all know I'm going through . . . ahem . . . a family crisis." Ukweli looked down and rubbed his hair.

"Well, we tried to tell you." Adam threw his hands up and then folded his arms.

"Yeah, I know. But, anyway, since things have been so chaotic at home, I just haven't thought about gathering you guys before I knew where Vasher was."

Charlotte said, "Do we have any idea how Vasher got to Kelley?"

"They monitored Alexander's movements, and once they got him, it was pretty easy to get her."

"Why didn't she call us in? Why did she go in alone?" Charlotte's voice quivered as she spoke.

"Either she didn't think she needed us, or she didn't think she had time."

Paul said, "Why didn't we get a trigger that there was activity here in the warehouse? How in the hell did they even get in here?"

"They were very thorough. They didn't just cut the feed. The system would've notified us. They replaced the feed and mimicked the signal. There was no way for us to know."

Charlotte said, "Wait, what about her life monitor? Surely her elevated heart rate would've been a trigger."

"They mimicked that too. See?" Ukweli held up a communicator and rotated the screen. "The system showed her vitals as normal until this morning. They must've jammed the signal to remove the chip."

Kei said, "They've been planning this for months."

"At least."

Adam said, "Do we know what they're going to do with Alexander? They obviously could've just killed him, so they must have plans for him."

"They do. I'm not sure what, though. We'll have to keep a close eye on Rome." The lack of information seemed to cause an increase in emotions.

"How are we going to get him back?" Charlotte began to cry.

"I don't know right now. We haven't had much luck tracking Vasher, so it will be difficult to find Alexander without knowing exactly what they have planned for him."

Paul said, "So now what?"

Everyone looked at Ukweli. Kelley had very specific burial requests, as did everyone on the team, but hers were considered bizarre and outrageous and the team wondered if Ukweli had intentions of fulfilling them.

Ukweli thought for a bit before he spoke. "We all have burial requests on file."

Kei said, "You can't be seriously thinking about doing that."

"What else can I do?"

Paul said, "We can take her to Chicago and bury her in her old neighborhood."

Charlotte stood. "We can take her to Okinawa and bury her with Remington Cross."

Ukweli looked at Charlotte with a raised brow. "Cross is buried in Okinawa? How do you know that?"

"That doesn't matter. I just think anything would be better than what you're planning."

"Guys, listen, I know it sounds crazy. Hell, it *is* crazy. But we all have end-of-life requests for a reason. Kelley chose this for herself, and it's my duty to honor it."

Kei shyly asked, "All of it?"

"To the letter."

"And when are you going to do this, UK?" Paul spoke, unable to hide his contempt and disbelief.

"Today. I'm not living another day with this hanging over my head. I've been dreading it this entire time."

Adam said, "Unbelievable. I'm with you, man, but you have to know this is a surfer's worst nightmare. I don't think I'll be able to watch."

"I won't hold that against you."

Charlotte said, "Wait, you're going to do this without Alexander getting a chance to say goodbye to her?" Again, she began to cry.

"Alexander already said goodbye to Kelley. He watched her die. Surely, he needs no further closure."

Ukweli stood on the deck of a small fishing vessel as it made its way out into the Gulf of Venice, located at the north end of the Adriatic Sea. Aside from the boat's captain and two mates, only Ukweli and Adam made the trip. Charlotte and Kei both refused to participate in Kelley's unorthodox burial at sea, and Paul was strictly forbidden by Kei from getting on the boat. As the ship grew closer to what Ukweli considered a suitable distance from shore, about twenty-five kilometers, Adam had a series of questions.

"So, we're doing this? We're actually doing this?"

"Adam, we're on the boat. We're headed out to sea. It's happening."

"Look, I know this is what Kelley requested, but surely she wrote that in jest, no?"

"I don't think she did. Besides, it doesn't matter what I think. It's not my place to wonder. It's my place to honor her wishes."

"Yeah, I get that. That's why I'm here. I still don't think I'll be able to watch, though."

"You don't have to." Ukweli was very stoic in his response to all of Adam's concerns.

Adam glanced at him from the side of his eye. "But you're going to watch it, huh?"

"That's the only way I can be sure it's done properly."

At that time, the captain of the ship rang a bell and yelled down to Ukweli, "This is far enough. The water's plenty deep for what you're aiming."

Ukweli yelled back, "Are you sure? If she washes up on shore, you'll regret it."

"I'm sure."

Ukweli looked at Adam. "It's time."

Adam sighed. "We're actually doing this."

"We're doing this. Grab that chum bucket."

Adam reluctantly grabbed one of the buckets filled with fish heads, guts, and blood, and began to scoop the contents into the ocean. The larger pieces slowly sank while the blood stayed on top of the water, creating a shiny red film. Adam guessed he would never forget the smell associated with his task here, but he knew Ukweli was right and he was proud to be a part of Kelley's final ceremony.

There are quite a few species of sharks that inhabit the Adriatic, and it didn't take long for some of the more aggressive ones to respond to the chum.

Adam looked into the water. "There's a couple of makos out there. They're pretty testy. I'm sure they'll get the job done.

"No, we can't trust makos. There have to be white sharks here. I'm not putting her out there until we see at least two white sharks."

It wasn't long before three large white sharks swam by the boat, first feeling out the situation, then becoming increasingly aggressive toward the other sharks.

"Okay, it's time." Ukweli stepped away from the rail.

"Unbelievable." Adam shook his head before joining him in the center of the boat.

Together they wrapped Kelley's body with several large stones to ensure she would sink. The stones weren't a part of her request, but Ukweli was determined to watch and just wasn't sure how much he would be able to stomach. The addition of the stones was in hopes that the most gruesome portions of the ceremony would take place below the surface and out of view. Ukweli took his chum bucket and saturated the linen with fish blood and small bits of flesh. The chum, like the stones, wasn't in Kelley's written request, but he hoped it would expedite the process. He emptied the contents of the bucket onto what looked like a blood-soaked mummy, and, with the help of the shipmates, Ukweli and Adam slid Kelley's body over the railing of the boat. There was a large splash as she hit the surface of the water.

Ukweli was terrified to see that the body didn't immediately sink and wondered if he had added enough rocks to be effective in such deep water. He was pleased to see the body rise vertically, like the *Titanic* as it had taken on water, and slowly sink into the bloody waves.

Adam turned his back on the sea. "I can't watch. I may be sick." His face turned a shade of light green.

Ukweli never looked away. He stared at the figure in the water as it slowly sank. He continued to stare even as he noticed a twenty-foot, two-ton great white shark approaching the sinking figure. He was startled by the speed at which the large female approached the body but couldn't make himself look away. His heart begged his body to turn, but his hands remained locked onto the railing and his eyes bugged as the shark, alone at first, then joined by multiple assailants, began to devour the body. Ukweli watched as long as he could before the activities mercifully descended to a more private depth.

Ukweli stepped down from a large wooden container. He didn't remember stepping onto it. Adam had been concerned that Ukweli might fall into the sea and become an unwilling participant in the frenzy, and had considered grabbing his waist, but couldn't bring himself to get close to the railing for fear he might see something that would revisit him in his nightmares. Ukweli turned to look at him.

"It's done."

"Are you okay?"

"I am, actually. It was my great honor to respect her wishes. Plus, it kind of reminded me of the *Transformers* movie when they buried Megatron . . ." Ukweli stopped abruptly.

"What is it, UK?" Ukweli stood silently for a few seconds. "UK, what is it?" Adam, concerned, placed his hand on Ukweli's shoulder.

Ukweli looked Adam in the eye. "I know how to find Vasher."

Ukweli grabbed his communicator and pressed a series of buttons. Mendoza eventually responded.

"UK, hey! How did everything go?"

"We'll talk later. I need you to get everyone to Atlanta. Forty-eight hours."

"Just your team?"

"And Miami."

Ukweli took one last glance at the water. There was still a red sheen on the surface and he wondered how much of it belonged to Kelley. She was one with the ocean now — just as she wished. *Thank you, Kelley.*

DECEMBER 28, 2050

Ukweli sat in the chair at the head of the large conference table in the office of the Church of the Seer in downtown Atlanta. Though he had recently done solo missions, this setting, surrounded by his team, made him feel comfortable. This was the best of the Seers, as it was meant to be. He took a moment to look around the room and admire the loyalty and character of the individuals around him. They were outstanding soldiers and good people. It had been nearly eight years since Remington Cross had assembled this team. There had been tragedies. They had lost Marcus and Calvin in Rome. They had lost Ava in the Dragon dimension as she saved Ukweli's life one last time. And, of course, the group continued to mourn the loss of Kelley in Venice. Still, the team showed great resolve in their desire to apprehend Vasher. Everyone now sat around the table waiting for marching orders from their leader. The team had begun to question whether Ukweli was focused enough to continue to lead missions. His resolve in completing Kelley's burial request had eased those concerns. He addressed the team in advance of a new mission.

"We've been struggling to apprehend Vasher because his cloaking devices have evaded our identification software and the radiation produced by his devices is too small to trigger our counters."

Charlotte responded first. "So, what makes you think you know how to find him now?"

"Burying Kelley at sea reminded me of a movie about alien robots when the government used a dam to conceal radiation. That's what Vasher has been doing."

"But that doesn't tell us where Vasher is. There are large dams all over the world. He could be hiding in any of them." Adam sounded intrigued but concerned.

"Were any of you watching when Jackson and Kiera married?" The room was silent and everyone shook their heads. "They were married in a resort on a lake in a small town. Everyone wondered why Jackson, the face of the Company, would choose a small-town lake instead of a luxury destination, or even one of his family's properties. The answer has been right in front of us all this time."

"Are you telling us Imperium has been using the dam in Hartwell to cloak radiation all this time?" Charlotte was skeptical.

"They have been producing a myriad of weapons and devices. The massive amount of concrete shields the radiation, while the output from the hydroelectric turbines mimics the energy production."

Kei cleared her throat and sat up in her chair. "So, we've been chasing Vasher all over the world, and all the while his base is ninety-eight miles from here?"

"That is correct."

"But wouldn't the government or law enforcement have figured this out by now?" Paul was a little annoyed and a little embarrassed.

"We have to remember that Imperium controlled all facets of government, including the corps of engineers."

Charlotte pulled up a scan of the dam and the surrounding area and placed it on the screen. "It's too open to make an assault. How are you planning on getting in?"

"That's why we need the Miami team. There is a bridge a few hundred yards downstream from the dam. Charlotte and Kei will set up sniper rifles there. Antonio, Trent, and Marianne will approach from the lakeside. You guys will take on heavy fire, so gear up. The attacks will draw out the security forces and Adam and Paul can go in after Vasher."

Paul was puzzled. "And where will you be?"

"If we are uncoordinated in our attack, we may prompt Vasher to blow the dam. In that case, anyone in the water or on the bridge will die."

"Unless?"

"Unless the kill switch is dismantled."

"And how do we dismantle the kill switch?"

"The easiest way would be to do it from inside the dam. Unfortunately, we won't have time to get inside to the switch before he blows the dam. The only other way is through the ventilation system."

"How can we get in?"

"We can't. It is only accessible from above the dam. It will require a sniper shot to destroy the hydrogen pump that cools the lines. The chain reaction will destroy the switch, but the shot must be made through a small vent."

"How small?"

"The diameter of the opening is about three feet." Ukweli held his hands up to display the width.

Kei said, "If there is no sniper post position above the dam, how can you make the shot?"

"I'll have to jump."

Charlotte was doubtful. "You're going to parachute onto the dam? That's suicide."

"It would be." Ukweli shook his head in agreement.

"Ukweli, are you saying you're going to shoot at a target that is three feet wide while you're in a freefall?"

"Can you think of another way? I'm open to suggestions."

"Is that even possible?"

"Yes. I've seen it done. Unfortunately, the only person who has ever done it is buried in the Adriatic."

"But if you miss the shot, we will all die?"

"I'll make the shot."

"What about one of the drones?"

"Even if we adapted a stealth drone with weapons capabilities, the space is too open. There wouldn't be enough time before their sensors read it."

"Ukweli . . ."

"I'll make the shot. But we have to be prepared to move at that moment. We'll only have seconds to get to Vasher once he knows we're there."

JANUARY 8, 2051

Ukweli sat in the middle of the craft as it sped from the airstrip in nearby Athens. The flight would be short, so he knew he would have to solidify his resolve before takeoff. Once the plane departed, he would have only a matter of minutes before reaching the jump site. He had jumped from planes before, no parachute. But he never had the added pressure of making a shot on the way down. This mission wouldn't be about strength, stamina, or perseverance. This would be a true test of skill. One shot, with the mission— and the lives of his team—hanging in the balance.

As the plane taxied on the runway, Ukweli closed his eyes and cleared his mind. There were no thoughts of Kiera and the sprouts. No thoughts of Mendoza and the baby. No thoughts of Kelley and the sharks. Just the mission. Clarity. Focus. He had never done this before. He never doubted he could, though. He was Captain Ukweli Aseyori for a reason. Plus, Thysia was his god. His confidence had never been higher.

He began to quote his favorite Bible verses as the plane grew closer to the jump site.

> *Blessed is the man who walks not in the counsel of the ungodly, nor stands in the way of sinners, nor sits in the seat of the scornful; but his delight is in the law of the Lord, and in his law doth he meditate day and night. He shall be like a tree planted by the rivers of water that brings forth his fruit in his season, His leaf also shall not wither; And whatsoever he doeth, shall prosper.*

"Ten seconds, sir!" Ukweli stood and placed his comm piece in his ear. He lightly touched the blue light on his shoulder. "Five."

Antonio, sitting on a watercraft in the big, open water of the lake, said, "That's the cue. Let's move." He, Trent, and Marianne twisted the throttles on their jet skis and moved slowly toward the dam.

Ukweli grabbed the latch on the door and quickly lifted it and slid it to the left. The door disappeared into the recess, exposing him to the incredible air pressure. His final thought before taking the leap out of the plane was that Coach Hassan and the Mongolian prime minister could never. He smiled and jumped into the darkness.

Ukweli had expected a mild wind, but found that there were strong gusts that threatened to push him off course. He had to make midair adjustments. His plan was to make the shot and land somewhere on the lake side of the dam. To land on the river side could mean trouble. The shallow water plus the hidden turbines provided real risk that he would rather avoid. He followed the readout on his goggles to stay in position to make the shot. He would deal with his landing situation as it came. If he landed poorly, it could cost him his life. If he missed the shot, his entire team could die.

He regulated his breathing as he fell. It helped to calm his heart rate. It gave him a better chance to make the impossible shot. A required breath at the wrong time could alter the path of the bullet by as much as eighteen inches. That's unacceptable when your target is only three feet wide.

He continued to adjust his trajectory until it was time to take the shot. Ukweli didn't care for shooting rifles. He preferred hand-to-hand combat, and he enjoyed using his sword. He shot pistols when guns were necessary. He always assigned sniper duties to someone else on his team. But in the event that he needed to make a long-distance shot, he generally used a modified Mk15. That rifle was far too heavy, though, for the freefall shot he was about to make. So, he opted for a custom Mk13. It was about a third of the weight with the range he needed to make the freefall shot at seven hundred meters. The bolt action wouldn't matter since he would only have one shot anyway.

His readout helped him adjust to the winds, but he would have to make the shot on his own. It would require all his training, things he had seen, physics and general theory, timing, trust, confidence, and perhaps, divine intervention.

Three seconds before the shot, Ukweli removed his earpiece, squared the rifle to his shoulder, took and held a breath, located the small vent via infrared imaging in his scope, and squeezed the trigger. The kickback from the rifle sent him into an uncontrolled spin, and by the time he regained control, he realized he was destined to land on the river side of the dam.

Charlotte watched from the bridge as the exhaust fire exploded from the small vent. There was immediate movement as gunfire rang out from different areas of the dam.

"Kei! Kei, come in!" Charlotte grabbed her binoculars and peered at the other side of the bridge where Kei was posted. She wasn't there.

Adam and Paul stood behind the largest of the above-ground generators just adjacent to the dam. There was a sprinkling of dead bodies that marked the path they took to the generator as they waited with great anticipation for the explosion from the vent signifying UK had indeed made the impossible shot. Once they received confirmation from Charlotte that the override switch had been disabled, they were free to move in.

Moving silently and quickly, the pair engaged and assaulted the surprised and terrified guardsmen. Paul led the attack and made his way up the circular stairs to the office of the overseer where Vasher sat. As Vasher looked on from his window, knowing there was no way for him to escape, he grabbed his pistol and emptied it into the staircase. He was knocked unconscious when the charge on the door exploded, giving Paul a clear entryway. When

Vasher woke up, he was securely tied to a chair with Adam and Paul seated on his desk, their guns pointed at his chest.

"We have Vasher secured," Paul spoke into the comms.

Charlotte responded. "Copy. Has anyone heard from Kei? She left her post on the bridge and hasn't checked back in."

Falling out of control and quickly moving off course, Ukweli realized it was much too late to adjust his landing target. The water on the river side of the dam was marked by the presence of large stone deposits, each representing immediate death if he landed on one of them. His only hope was to land in the deeper water closest to the dam. That's where the underwater turbines were. It would give him a chance.

As he got closer to the water and closer to the dam, he turned his rifle vertical and threw it down with all his might. He would need the weight of the rifle to break the surface of the water before he landed. Otherwise, he may as well land on the rocks. As the butt of the rifle broke through the surface, Ukweli, having just seconds ago been safe inside the cargo plane, landed feet first in the Savannah River, fifteen feet from the dam. The impact of the landing momentarily knocked him unconscious. He regained consciousness three minutes later on the South Carolina side of the riverbank, on his back, coughing up water. He slowly opened his eyes as water dripped from Kei's face onto his.

"You're one lucky bastard, Captain."

"Do we have Vasher?"

"Yes, sir."

"Let's move."

"Yes, sir."

Ukweli rolled off Kei's lap onto all fours and attempted to stand when he felt a sharp pain in his lower left leg. He reached down to assess the damage. His fractured ankle had already begun to swell.

"Dammit." He hobbled a few steps.

"You okay, sir?"

Ukweli grunted and stood straight. "I'll be fine. Let's get to the rendezvous point."

The generators being run at night had saved Ukweli's life and provided a riverside deep-water landing point. It had also made it so they couldn't cross the river to the rendezvous point without going across the bridge. Ukweli couldn't run, but his pride wouldn't allow him to request a transport. So, he and Kei retraced her steps and walked up the hill, through the forest, and across the bridge to the meeting location. There he found Adam, Paul, and Charlotte standing next to a bound and gagged Vasher.

Ukweli looked around. "Where are the others?"

Paul spoke up. "Headed back to Athens. I told them you might not want them here for this."

Ukweli tried to take a knee in front of Vasher, but there was no flexibility in his ankle, so he just stood. He removed the tie and gag. Vasher took a deep breath.

"Congrats, Captain. You've finally succeeded." Vasher's voice was muffled and scratchy.

"Congrats to you as well, Vasher. You've been hard to catch."

"Now what? What are your plans? Sure, you could kill me. But what does that accomplish?"

"You're the final link to Imperium. With you gone, the

war will end for good, and I can rest. The whole world can finally rest."

Vasher looked at Ukweli with a curious grin and started to laugh hysterically. It was a genuine laugh that centered around his abdomen. The team watched silently.

"You think . . . you've been thinking . . . that this is about Imperium?" He continued to laugh out loud.

Ukweli looked around at his team and then back at Vasher. "Isn't it?"

Vasher could hardly speak for laughing. "Yazata was in your home and you still think this is about Imperium!"

Charlotte asked, "Who is Yazata?"

Ukweli said, "Vasher, what the hell are you talking about?"

Vasher abruptly stopped laughing and attempted to stand. Adam firmly placed his hand on his shoulder to encourage him to remain on his knees. "To be so damn gifted, you're the most arrogant, obtuse son of a bitch alive!" He paused and looked up at Ukweli. "The goddess is rising."

Ukweli closed his eyes. "Mithras."

"Who is Mithras?" Kei asked.

Ukweli didn't answer her. "What is her plan?"

Vasher began to laugh again. "It doesn't matter. You're already too late. She cannot be stopped. You should've joined her when she gave you the chance."

Adam was concerned. He'd seen that look in Ukweli's eyes before. "Ukweli . . . Take it easy, man."

Vasher continued to laugh. "And to think, all this time, you've been chasing me thinking it would end the war. The war has only just begun!"

Kei was also concerned that Ukweli's countenance was changing. "UK . . . we don't have Alexander yet."

"It must be frustrating to think you're so close." Vasher continued to laugh. "Kelley is gone. You'll never see the priest again. The war will never end. Face it, Captain. You've lost. Your efforts have been in vain. You've stopped nothing. Your entire life has been a strenuous exercise in futility."

Paul placed his hand on Ukweli's shoulder. "Hey, big guy, don't listen to him."

Ukweli shoved Paul away. He grabbed Vasher by the collar and lifted him off the ground, pulling his dagger from its holding place near his right leg. "Tell Kelley hello for me." He drove the dagger into the underside of Vasher's chin, through his throat and into the back of his head. He pulled him closer and watched as he flailed and gasped for air. Ukweli stood with a blank expression and slowly removed the blade from Vasher's head. The blood ran down onto his hands. As Vasher's face fell, Ukweli ran the sides of his blade through Vasher's hair to clean the blood before replacing the dagger in its holster.

Ukweli threw Vasher's body to the ground and walked toward the transport. He was immediately reminded that his ankle was cracked, but he refused to honor Vasher with a show of vulnerability. He calmly walked to the van, opened the door, and sat down in the second seat.

Antonio, Trent, and Marianne emerged from the forest where they had been hiding. They had heard stories about Ukweli's ruthlessness and were curious to know if he could resist avenging Kelley after pursuing Vasher for so long. They had learned he could not. Or maybe he could, but consciously chose not to. Either way, it made them fear him, and they began to question if the Church of the Seer remained in line with the original tenants. They also began to question if Captain Aseyori remained loyal to Thysia. His brutal, emotionless execution of Vasher suggested otherwise.

JANUARY 8, 2051

Ukweli sat on a large, padded table in the basement of the Church of the Seer headquarters building in downtown Atlanta. He had just completed the barrage of scans on his ankle that confirmed a torn ligament and two fractures. Considering the feat, though, he was proud of himself. If a busted ankle was the worst of it, he considered it well worth it to have seen the life drain from Vasher's face. He would replay that image in his mind several times over the next few days, and it made him smile each time.

Ukweli was fitted with a mechanized walking sleeve to relieve the pressure on his ankle and facilitate the healing process. He remembered how his father had once worn a large boot on his leg when he tore his Achilles tendon, and Ukweli was grateful that technology had long surpassed that archaic age of medicine.

Ukweli headed upstairs to the office to check in with Charlotte before heading home. This would be the first time he would board the plane on the high of a successful mission. Vasher had taken Kelley and led him on a worldwide pursuit, and he could now breathe a sigh of relief. Or could he? Alexander was still missing. Vasher had said his mission wasn't about Imperium. Of course, he could be lying. Why would Vasher be honest about his sinister plans? Then again, what reason did he have to lie? His life was all but over, yet he had taken his last moments to gloat about the goddess and her plans. Ukweli decided it could wait. It could all wait. He had buried Kelley. He had killed Vasher. Imperium was defeated. The Church of the Seer had prevailed. He had won. It was over.

Now, he could return to Zurich with a clear mind and focus on his family and his future. He needed rest. His team needed rest. They had earned it.

8

DYSFUNCTION

Kirsten Gabrielle Aseyori was born in Zurich. Mendoza was exhausted and happy. Ukweli was cautiously happy. Kiera hated Mendoza, but immediately fell in love with Gabby. PonyTail knew Mendoza loved Ukweli, but he loved Mendoza and Gabby anyway. PonyTail was afraid of Ukweli.

It was PonyTail's intention to move Mendoza and Gabby back to Atlanta, but she refused to leave Zurich. Ukweli made it clear that it was his wish that she stay in Zurich so he could be closer to Gabby, but he understood if she wanted to move on with her life. She had absolutely no intention of moving anywhere Ukweli wasn't. Kiera knew this. PonyTail accepted this.

PonyTail insisted on making the rental payments at Mendoza's apartment and demanded a level of independence from Ukweli's hovering eye. Ukweli agreed to give Mendoza *her* desired level of personal independence as long as it didn't restrict his access to Gabby. Kiera wished

Mendoza and PonyTail could fade into the clouds in some other part of the world, or afterworld, and leave Gabby with her. Since Mendoza wouldn't leave, PonyTail abandoned his remaining tour dates to spend what was left of the spring in Zurich. He wanted to be helpful, but mostly he wanted Mendoza to take him seriously. He found himself being given more chores than influence.

"I'm just saying I don't understand. What do you see in this guy?" PonyTail sat on the edge of the bed with his arm resting on a basket of baby clothes.

"PT, we've been through this before." Mendoza stood in front of the basket and sorted through the tiny garments.

"I mean, he's a good-looking dude, but he has some serious baggage."

"Please don't."

"Claire, he's married. And his wife is a damn smoke show. And they've known each other since they were teens. And she had two of his children."

"PT, I know all that. You're not presenting any new information." Mendoza spoke without looking away from the basket.

"And he's obviously a pimp in these streets. He cheated on his first wife with his current wife, and then he cheated on his current wife with you. Not to mention all those chicks in London, and around the world, when he was playing soccer."

"Look, since you've got so much to say, at least fold these clothes while you talk. It's gonna take me all day to sort through these things."

PonyTail reached into the basket and grabbed a pink onesie with a small purple crown on the front. "And the people he's killed! Who knows when he might snap!"

Mendoza dropped her head and sighed. "Look, I've

never said he is without flaws. There's a dark side to him, but I can't help that I fell in love with him. Maybe he's not good for me, and no, he's not available at the moment, but Gabby is here and we're certainly safer when UK is around. Surely even you must understand that."

"I get it, I really do. But I've been chasing you for years now, and you keep shutting me out for the remote possibility that you could be with a womanizing killer. I mean, I may not be much in Switzerland, but I'm pretty hot in the States. A lot of Southern girls would love to be in your shoes."

Mendoza reached out to hug PonyTail and gave him a kiss. "PT, you know I'm crazy about you. I trust you and I'm glad you're here. That has to be enough for right now though."

"Yeah, I hear you." PonyTail kept folding.

"And when it comes to UK, you know I'm a big girl. I can take care of myself."

"You know, I'm starting to think I might want Pax in a different program." Ukweli popped a few kernels of popcorn in his mouth.

"Cut the crap, UK. Brad runs the best youth football program in Zurich and Pax can play with his friends. We're not moving him."

"See? That's what I mean. Why can't you just call him Coach Hassan like everybody else? Why does he have to be Brad?"

"That's his name, UK."

"Well, just know this—if I ever get the suspicion he's laid a hand on you, they'll have to call in for dental records to identify him."

"Yes, Ukweli, I'm familiar with you."

"Look, I'm not trying to be crude, but it's the principle. This nonsense with Claire aside, you know I don't play about mine."

"Oh, it's the double standard for me, though. Why is it okay for you to call her Claire, but not okay for me to call him Brad? You brought a whole baby up in my house, but you got something to say about how I refer to the coach?"

"Apples and oranges, love. Besides, you're crazy about Gabby."

"Nah, this ain't about Gabby. You did your dirt and now you don't trust me."

"Babe, I trust you explicitly. I trust you with my life and the lives of my children. I don't trust Hassan."

"UK, he's just a coach. That's it."

"Nah, there's something there. I haven't put my finger on it yet. I'll figure it out, though. In the meantime, if he shows up at my house again, I'll consider it a hostile act."

Kiera pinched Ukweli's cheeks. "Aww, that's adorable. My little jealous baby." She kissed him and grabbed a handful of popcorn.

⑨

INTRODUCTION (THE FIRST ONE)

NOVEMBER 23, 2051

Alexander sat in his assigned room, 5444, of the Connaught Hotel in Manhattan. It had been almost a year since he left that room. His entire existence took place in that room. There were people who brought him three meals daily, and two snacks, in that room. There was a personal trainer who took him through a strenuous workout six days per week in that room. There were speech coaches who tutored him in Greek and Mandarin in that room. There were professors who taught him randomized algorithms, discrete probability, and stochastic calculus in that room. He was groomed daily in that room. And when he had questions concerning his inability to leave, he was connected to an electrical device and tortured in that room. Eventually, Alexander stopped asking questions.

When it was time for lunch, Alexander noticed the usual meal arrangement was now set up for two. He simply took a seat at the table and waited to see who would occupy the second seat. Tom was one of several attendants who saw to Alexander's needs.

"Good afternoon, Tom." Alexander adjusted his napkin in his lap.

"Happy Thanksgiving, sir. You'll be really pleased with this meal. The chef has spared no expense."

"Thank you, Tom. I'm sure I will. And happy Thanksgiving to you." Alexander smiled pleasantly.

"Just a heads-up, sir, you will have a lunch guest today."

"Fine. I'll wait before I get started."

"No, sir. She has requested that you go ahead with your meal. She'll join you when she's available."

"So be it."

Tom lifted the lid on the silver tray to reveal a large turkey roasted to perfection with seven small porcelain plates with assorted side dishes.

"What portion of the entrée would you take, sir?"

"Hmm, I'll just take the most appropriate cut, Tom."

"Very well, sir." Tom held out his utensils and began to slice the turkey from the breast down. He placed a large slice of turkey on Alexander's plate along with dressing and gravy, macaroni and cheese, green beans, cranberry sauce, candied yams with marshmallows, and a piece of cornbread covered in butter and honey.

"Well, this looks magnificent. Thank you, Tom."

"Yes, sir. Your guest will arrive momentarily. Until then, enjoy your lunch, sir." There was a knock at the door. "Well, it seems your guest has arrived. It is appropriate to stand."

Alexander placed his utensils on the table beside his plate, wiped his mouth with his napkin, and stood. Tom nervously walked to the door, turned to look at Alexander, then opened it. A beautiful woman walked slowly, regally, into the room.

"Welcome, goddess."

"Thank you, Tom. That will be all for now." Tom bowed and quickly left the room. Alexander stood silently, but even he noticed how beautiful the woman was. "Alexander, please, sit. Continue your meal."

"Thank you."

"Alexander, I hope you know I have such a great deal of respect for you."

"Thank you."

"You've been through so much, yet you continue, day by day, to improve yourself."

"Thank you."

"And might I say, you look amazing. The trainers have truly outdone themselves."

"Thank you."

"Goodness, what exactly have we done to you?"

"I am well cared for. I have everything I need."

"Oh no, this won't do at all. You see, Alexander, I need your obedience *and* your passion. Obedience alone simply won't do. We must sell the movement. You, Alexander, you must sell the movement."

"I apologize. I don't understand."

"Alexander, please allow me to introduce myself. I am Mithras." The goddess touched Alexander on the forehead and his mind was transported to the stars, where he was given a vision of the goddess receiving cosmic power. He was captivated and began to cry at the breadth of knowledge and power the goddess possessed. Alexander's eyes, light brown at birth, suddenly turned icy blue.

"I am here to do the bidding of Mithras. Please tell me how I can serve you?"

"Alexander, in the beginning of time, the beginning of your galaxy as you have come to know it, my father fought a battle for the souls of this world, your world, the world he created for his pleasure and his glory. My father defeated a sinister foe and banished him from the throne room. Since those times, the Magician and his followers have sought to flood your world with lies. He has been successful at using his deranged captives to create division through unrealistic expectations. Some of his lies have led to broken homes, depression, anxiety, and guilt. Other lies have led to wars and the loss of many lives. Yet the message of the Magician continues to thrive as his lies have led the masses to abandon the truth in favor of the unfulfilled promises made by the followers of the Way. I have come, in honor of my father, the creator and rightful ruler of this world, the angel of light, to provide a chance for mankind to get it right. I will show all men, as I have shown you, that my father is the one true god of this world and only through him can we redeem its citizens."

Alexander wept as he was given visions of the lowest moments of his life. He saw the door of the closet as he hid from his molester. He saw the face of Pope Incursus as he lay dying in the backseat of the papal sedan. He saw Kelley's neck go limp as the sound of the gunshot rang in his ears and her chin rested on the gray tape that bound her torso to the chair. Alexander made a fist and squeezed so aggressively that his palms began to bleed. "I have been under the influence of the Magician and his lies for far too long. Let us go into the world and set the captives free!"

Mithras smiled. "Much better." Yazata appeared and bowed at the feet of the goddess.

(10)

SKILL DEVELOPMENT

Though Pax was a year younger than Dakota and two years younger than Bryce, he was already the best player on the Alpine Marmot Under-10. Pax was known to take team practices very seriously, and Ukweli added lights to his training area in the backyard because Pax often got up in the middle of the night or early in the morning to train alone. He enjoyed training in the rain or in freezing temperatures, as he felt it gave him a mental edge over the other boys. He approached his team drill sessions with unflappable focus. This particular practice, though, he had a separate agenda. He paid close attention to the movements, results, and reactions of all his teammates in the line as they practiced penalty shots. He saw Dakota calmly place his first shot in the upper right-hand corner of the net.

"Attaboy, Kota!" Coach Hassan jogged over and gave Dakota a high five.

Bryce was next, and though the keeper guessed correctly, the shot was flawless and slid just under the keeper's fluorescent glove.

"Whew! Nice shot, Bryce!" Coach Hassan was impressed.

Pax never missed penalty opportunities, so everyone was shocked when he stepped to the ball and his shot went high and wide left. Coach Hassan was most surprised of all.

"Pax, what was that?"

"My bad, Coach."

"My bad? That wasn't even close!"

"Yes, sir."

"Haven't I told you all that penalties require focus?"

"Yes, sir."

"It's not just muscle memory. It's strategy. It's learning. And most of all, it requires intentionality. You must always be present. That was a wasted rep."

"Yes, sir."

"Don't 'yes sir' me. Hit a lap and come back and try it again."

Pax dropped his head and began a slow jog toward the edge of the field away from the line. When he felt he was far enough away, he reached into his pocket and pulled out the silver dollar. He stopped jogging long enough to give the coin a flip. As the coin started on its way down, Pax once again experienced the horizontal whirling of the environment, the sky and trees and people blending as if smeared streaks of paint, only this time he was violently snatched from his place on the edge of the field, as if by a great hand, and placed back in the line in time to see Bryce take his penalty.

"Whew! Nice shot, Bryce!"

Pax stepped to the ball and shot it right down the middle of the net. The keeper dove hard to the left.

"Cool as a cucumber. No worries." Coach Hassan patted

Pax on the top of his head as he jogged to the back of the line.

Pax would repeat the flip of the coin two more times during the practice session to determine how far into the past each flip would take him. His results inconclusive, he decided, for the moment, that each flip would return him to an instant in time, within a set of parameters, that was consistent with his thoughts. He could simply think of a moment, within a certain time range, flip the coin, and be returned to that moment in the recent past. No one seemed aware of the recurrence, and Pax allowed himself to be moderately excited about the implications of time travel on the world of physics. In his mind, although not through algebraic topology, he had personal proof of Einstein's "dilations." What he lacked, perhaps due to immaturity or overexcitement, was an awareness of the immense implications of possessing such cosmic abilities, and furthermore, who, or what, might be drawn to the waves in the wake of a temporal anomaly.

"So, this has been confirmed?"

"Yes. This is the same disturbance that has occurred multiple times over the last year. Since last December."

"And the disturbance has been consistent?"

"Yes, six seconds each time."

"And how many times has it happened?"

"Eleven times before today. Three times today makes fourteen in all."

"From the same source?"

"Yes. It seems the weapon is growing more comfortable using his abilities."

"Is he using a conduit?"

"Yes, a vintage coin."

"But no more than six seconds?"

"No more or less. It seems he is still not aware of his true capabilities."

"And the man remains unaware? The other Seers?"

"It seems that way, yes."

"I think the boy is too dangerous to leave alive."

"The goddess won't have it. She has a greater purpose for him."

"But if the Seers ever learn . . ."

"They will eventually. That's why we mustn't fail."

"So should we mobilize now?"

"No. Let's wait until the goddess makes her announcement. That will draw his father away. We'll move then. Just be sure everything—and everyone—is in place."

11

THE ANNOUNCEMENT

DECEMBER 24, 2051

This was a very different December holiday season for Ukweli. He wasn't under the strain of looking for Vasher. Kiera and Mendoza, along with the invaluable contributions of Mrs. Bergstrom, seemed to have found a happy medium concerning the rearing of the children. Kiera still didn't like Mendoza; she never would, for understandable reasons. She did, however, adore Gabby and it was worth it to Kiera to put up with Mendoza in her life if it meant she got to love on Gabby. Mendoza appreciated Kiera's love for Gabby because it gave her what she so desperately wanted—access, even if limited, to Ukweli. Mrs. Bergstrom was always there to serve as judge, referee, or mediator whenever conflicts inevitably arose.

Ukweli sat at a large table inside The Hiker's Landing, a bar and grille a few miles from his home. He looked across the table at Adam, who was busy with his third tequila shot with two others sitting on the table waiting their turn. Ukweli didn't care for pub grub, especially the way the Swiss did it, but he had learned to appreciate the art of the wing, specifically crispy spicy lemon pepper flats, the way they did it in Atlanta. While these certainly were no Atlanta wings, they were better than jackfruit and falafel.

"UK, seriously, take a shot with me."

"You seem to have things well under control."

"This tequila is so smooth, man. Twice the buzz with half the burn."

"You got it. Enjoy."

"What's the deal, bruv? It's Yuletide Eve. Vasher is dead. Your plane crash of a family seems to have miraculously gained some measure of stability. What could possibly be eating at you right now?"

"I'm fine. I'm here, right?"

"You here but you're not here. Seriously, what's the problem?" Adam seemed genuinely concerned.

"Look, I've told you before, I'm fine. This just isn't my kind of atmosphere."

"This is fun! Sports on the television. Hot food and cold drinks. Plus, the servers here are just my type."

"I have enough complications at home. No need adding to it."

"I said my type, not yours. You could be my wingman, though."

"You don't need a wingman."

"I certainly don't. But you need to *be* a wingman. You seem like you've gotten stagnant. I'm here to help."

"I'm just fine. I love my life."

"Tell your face."

"Look, maybe you should consider settling down."

"You want me to trade my life for yours? Nah, I'm good.

I'm just here to hang out with my homeboy, enjoy the holiday festivities, and explore a few of these Swiss mountain peaks, if you know what I mean." Adam flashed a devilish, pearly-white grin.

"Everybody knows what you mean, Adam."

Ukweli put a chicken wing to his mouth and took a bite. He took a moment to notice his surroundings. In his earlier days, he would've been as eager as Adam to take advantage of the bevy of beautiful blondes currently occupying the pub. But now, he found himself wondering how often they changed out the cooking oil. *Not often enough,* he thought.

"How are the kids? I can't wait to see them. It's been a while."

"They should be back in an hour or so. We'll head to the house then. They miss Uncle Adam."

"Pax has really grown. He's gonna be tall."

"Doctors say as tall as me, or taller." Ukweli paused and swallowed. "Hey, have you ever had the feeling that something bad was about to happen?"

"Goodness, here we go. You and your intuition."

"No, nothing like that. I've just been having these dreams about Alexander. I'm sure he's still alive, but there's always a dark cloud over him in my dreams. I can't tell what's coming, but it seems bad."

"Alexander will turn up. Charlotte mans the web constantly. She'll find him."

"That's the problem. I'm not sure what she's gonna find."

"You're starting to sound loco, man. I told you not to watch Kelley in that ocean, but you insisted. You seriously need to seek counseling. There's no way that didn't affect you."

"This isn't about that. This is something else entirely. I don't know what it has to do with Alexander, but it's keeping me awake at night."

"You just can't allow yourself to be happy, can you? You said yourself that things are as good as they can be at home, yet you still find something to worry yourself about. Please, just let it go before you talk something up."

As Adam was finishing his sentence, four of the televisions in the pub went to a black screen with the words "Special Announcement" written in bold red. The screen faded to a video feed of a podium and the bottom tagline read "London Mithraeum." A small crowd of reporters gathered around and there was only one microphone on the stand. Ukweli watched the screen curiously as Adam finished the last shot of tequila and smacked his lips.

"What is this about?" Ukweli pointed to the nearest television screen.

"I'm sitting here with you, UK. I don't know any more about it than you do. Besides, it's probably just President James announcing a fifth term." Ukweli chuckled at the bizarre nature of it all.

After two or three minutes, President James stepped to the podium.

Ukweli looked at Adam and said, "Nailed it." They both laughed. "Why is he announcing from London, though?" Ukweli was solemn again. "And why would he announce from that location? Didn't we track Vasher there once?"

Adam squinted. "Yeah, I think you're right. That place does look familiar somehow." He began to wipe his face.

Ukweli had already cleaned and sanitized his hands. He gestured to the barman. "Hey, turn that up." The barman grabbed a remote control and adjusted the volume on the third set from the left.

President James was dressed officially. He wore a gray suit with a bright red tie and two lapel pins near his left collar, one an American flag and one that looked like the sun. His hair was groomed, a little more gel than usual. His black beard showed distinguished signs of graying, and his eyes were bright and his posture confident.

"My fellow citizens of Earth, I bring you joyous greetings in this December holiday season from the hallowed ground of the London Mithraeum. It is here, in this most honored of locations, that the leaders of the free world, eleven men including myself, have gathered what is undoubtedly the most consequential assembly of our generation."

Ukweli touched the collar of his shirt. "Charlotte."

"I see it."

"What is this?"

"I don't know. I didn't know they were there."

President James continued, "Over the course of the last two thousand-plus years, our world has seen incredible changes. Empires have emerged from Egypt to Persia, the Romans, the Han, the Ottoman, and even now we in America have unprecedented military might. Yet we do not exercise these abilities as we could because of our intense appreciation for all of humanity. We believe it is the right, indeed the God-given right, of each and every citizen of each and every sovereign nation to live free from tyranny, oppression, and fear with the freedom that comes with being made in the image of God. Free to live as one chooses. Free to love. Free to worship. Free to pursue dreams. Free to grow. These are the ideals which have been pursued since humans first inhabited this planet. And yet, we have failed. So often, we have failed. So consistently, we have failed. And why? Why have the citizens of this planet so consistently failed to live up to the standard set by almighty God? It's simple. Greed. In fact, we have accomplished little more than war and human suffering in our thousands of years here. And as one empire would fall only to be replaced by a rising empire with even greater moral deficiency and corruption, we continued to spiral into the depths of famine and failure, all because of greed."

"Charlotte?"

"It's him, and he is actually in London."

"Why didn't we know?"

"Good question."

"And so now, it is with humility and great pride that I am able to stand before you as a representative of the newly formed World Society to introduce you to our chairman. This is the man who has done what no other world leader has been able to accomplish in history. I am pleased to introduce to the world the Chairman of the Board, Alexander Scott!"

Ukweli and Adam watched in stunned silence as Alexander shook hands with President James and approached the microphone.

Charlotte came through on the comms. "Scan confirmed. It's him."

"Ladies and gentlemen, citizens of our great world, welcome to the future! Today I stand before you as a recipient of the unmerited grace and favor bestowed upon me by the heir of the universe. The goddess Mithras in her infinite wisdom has chosen to bless our world with the peace that no other leader in history, no other deity in existence, has been able to deliver. Our goddess has blessed us with, for the first time ever, a treaty of nations, newly coined the World Society, that recognizes the sovereignty and established borders of one hundred and ninety-eight nations, all of whom, as agreed upon by their regional representatives, swear to protect the peace in our world."

Adam looked puzzled. "Has he been working out?" Ukweli shushed him and continued to stare at the screen.

Alexander continued, "Every nation has agreed to the borders as outlined in the World Society covenant, and as such in this moment, no nation is a threat to the culture or safety of any other nation on this planet. Furthermore, in the event of any interplanetary conflicts, all nations have agreed to convene as one world. Our world. Your world. I am honored to play a small role in the present global peace, just as our goddess intended. Thank you, and goddess bless!"

As Alexander stepped away from the podium, the eleven world leaders all lined up to greet the chairman. President James was first in line. He shook Alexander's hand, bowed in a show of humility, and proceeded to kiss the large diamond-encrusted ring on Alexander's right hand. The other leaders followed suit, each with a shake, bow, and kiss.

Ukweli sat in the basement of his home surrounded by three large display screens. Adam sat beside him and watched as he contacted Charlotte.

"Did you find Paul and Kei?"

"Yes, I'm patching them through now."

Charlotte appeared on the screen along with Paul and Kei.

Ukweli spoke first. "Well, I guess we know where Alexander is."

"He seems to be taking good care of himself." Adam was impressed.

Charlotte sounded concerned. "What do we know about the goddess Mithras, aside from what we can learn from the search engines?"

Ukweli blushed but realized the need for transparency in this moment. "This is the deity Vasher spoke about in Hartwell. I haven't had the pleasure of meeting this goddess face to face, but I have met one of her representatives. It was formidable."

Kei spoke. "What is their angle? Is the World Society just a replacement for Imperium?"

Charlotte responded. "It's possible. I'm curious to see if they reboot the Torqueo Anima project. We'll have to wait and see what kind of authority they have given themselves. I'll try to get a download of the treaty. We should start with a description of powers given to the chairman and the . . . wait . . . Ukweli, we have a call coming in." Charlotte pressed a sequence of buttons and raised one eyebrow. "It's Alexander."

"Patch him through." Ukweli leaned forward in his seat.

As the cleanly shaven face of Alexander Scott appeared on the screen, there were mixed responses among the Seers. Paul, Kei, and Adam were all thrilled and immediately expressed excitement at seeing Alexander safe and doing well. They had been searching for him ever since Vasher had executed Kelley in front of him, almost a year ago to the day, and they all allowed themselves to be happy for him in the moment. Charlotte was also happy to see Alexander alive and well, but she was concerned about his motives. She was the only one who knew that the software from the World Society was attempting to hack the server in Atlanta. She was also the only one who noticed that Alexander's eyes were blue.

Ukweli had unique knowledge of the goddess Mithras, given his encounters with the demon Yazata. He had been informed that Mithras inhabited his dark passions, a concept he didn't fully understand, but he had been a Seer long enough to know Alexander's involvement with Mithras, much like with Vasher, would end up being a challenge for the Seers.

Alexander addressed the group from a large seat in his private plane. He wore a dark-gray dress shirt with a black tie, and his sleeves were rolled halfway up his forearms. "Good evening, friends. It's so good to see you all."

Ukweli spoke through the friendly greetings from the other Seers. "It's good to see you well, Alexander. You look healthy."

"I'm as fit as a fiddle, UK. I have eternal purpose in my life. That makes a big difference."

"Did you not have purpose before? In your service to Thysia?"

"I found purpose in gleaning from Incursus. I found purpose in loving my wife. My love for Kelley was my comfort for all the times he failed me. My service to the Magician swallowed years of my life, but I'm finally on the straight and narrow."

Ukweli felt his stomach sink, but his expression remained sober. "The Magician? Alexander, that's the language of Imperium."

"UK, that's the language of the truth. But I didn't call for a theological debate. I have a much gentler, nobler reason for reaching out, aside from missing you all terribly."

"Carry on."

"It is the position of the World Society that the agents of the Church of the Seer have served this planet with courage and excellence. You have fought off the forces of evil for years with basically no recognition, and the Board of the Eleven would like to correct that."

"What do you mean?"

"It is the opinion of the Board that the agents of the

Church of the Seer are no longer needed to patrol the world. With the destruction of Imperium, thanks to you, there are no more demons to slay. No more torqs to hunt. With the one hundred ninety-eight signatures on the treaty of nations, there are no more governments to topple. Neither Ann Jefferson nor Jennifer Devore remains on this planet to cause you trouble. Vasher is dead and the World Society has nothing but admiration for you. That is why we seek only to honor you and your courageous comrades, and to give you the freedom to return home to your beautiful wife and your adorable children for good. We will also give my darling Kelley a fitting memorial."

"What's the catch?"

"I know it is in your nature not to trust, but there is no catch. You, your team, and your family and friends will come to London, where we will honor you for your years of service to our planet. Afterward, you can all just go home and enjoy your lives in our new peace."

"So now that you have complete control of the planet, you're just going to turn it over to the Board?"

"That is the will of Mithras. I'm honored to be her chosen vessel."

"Hmm."

"Look, I have to run. I'll send you the details. It has been a pleasure. I'm so glad to see you all doing well. I'll be in touch." His call ended. The feed was silent.

"How long will it take you guys to get to Atlanta?"

Pax didn't ask for any December holiday season gifts. In fact, he insisted that his mother not buy him anything and asked her, instead, to donate to the Eleonore Foundation, which supported the Children's Hospital of Zurich. She compromised by purchasing him a new microscope and a new pair of soccer cleats. She also carefully fitted a receipt for a one-thousand-dollar donation to the hospital in his name in his stocking along with protein bars and post-work hydration packets. Pax didn't eat candy.

There were, however, plenty of gifts around the tree, as Kip had a very long and specific list. Kiera made the mistake of letting her have access to the massive catalog from the large toy store in town, and Kip would not let this opportunity pass. She figured she wouldn't get everything she pointed at, but even a portion would serve her well. She was not disappointed.

Gabby had a few boxes under the tree. Kiera couldn't stand the thought of her not having gifts to open. Though she couldn't do much more than pull at the ribbons, it made Kiera smile. Mendoza was happy that Kiera was happy. She knew a happy Kiera meant a happy Ukweli, and a happy Ukweli was a vulnerable Ukweli. Mendoza looked forward to traveling to Atlanta with the team. She didn't care about Alexander. She barely knew him. But she was growing weary of waiting for time with Ukweli, and she hoped Atlanta would provide a window.

Mendoza spent time with Kip and her harvest of toys so Kiera could spend time with Gabby uninterrupted. Ukweli and Pax trained.

Mrs. Bergstrom prepared traditional holiday dishes: köttbullar, Janssons frestelse, and prinskorv, along with honey ham and Southern side dishes. The fare and the cinnamon apple cider made the whole house smell like the holidays. Everyone was content. Everyone did what they wanted to do.

(12)

INTRODUCTION (THE SECOND ONE)

Ukweli opened the curtains revealing the large balcony that opened toward the west. There was a stunning view of the Atlanta cityscape as the sun began to set behind the sharp peaks of the skyscrapers. The skyline reflected the development of the economy of the city, which had grown immensely during Ukweli's time with the Seers. He slid the glass door to the side and stepped out onto the concrete base. He took a deep breath and rested his hands on the edge of the rail and allowed himself to feel a sense of peace. He hadn't known this feeling for quite some time, and now it seemed to be a regular part of life. Peace. Agitating peace. He was slightly startled when Mendoza walked up and hugged him from behind. She squeezed him tightly and rested her cheek in the middle of his back.

"What are you out here thinking about?"

"Nothing."

"Liar."

"No, seriously. For the first time in so long, there is peace in my life."

"And you're wondering why you're annoyed?"

Ukweli scrunched his face and turned around. "How could you possibly know that?"

"I know you." She tapped his cheek.

"Do you have any answers?"

"You've been on a mission since you were a child. You've never known a life without one. Honestly, men need a mission. You need a conquest."

"Do you count?" He chuckled.

"I'm not a conquest, Ukweli." Mendoza did not chuckle.

"You sure? Because . . ."

"Yes, I'm sure." She released him and stepped back into the bedroom.

"I'm joking." Ukweli walked toward the room but stayed on the balcony in the mild sunlight. "But don't people work hard so they can enjoy a sense of peace? When do I get to rest on my laurels?" He noticed he was speaking with his hands, so he turned again to face the rail.

"You're not built that way. You're a conqueror. You're a warrior. Warriors fight. Kings go out to battle."

Ukweli searched for animal shapes in the clouds but didn't see any. "But I have so much to lose now."

"Then it's even more important that you fight."

"You're only saying that because you're attracted to that part of me."

"Ukweli, I'm in love with all of you. I'm saying that because I want you to be who you truly are. I'm not trying to change you."

"That's certainly not what Kiera would say."

"Kiera wants what is best for Kiera. She's always been about herself."

Ukweli glanced at her over his shoulder. "That's not fair."

"That's the truth." Mendoza shrugged.

"She just wants me there for the sprouts. Is that so bad?"

"And I want you around for Gabby. But I knew who you were when I fell for you. So did she. The difference is she wants you tame and domesticated. She wants you there to serve her and her needs. I want you just the way you are. I want the passion, the danger, the intensity—"

"The sex."

"The fact that you're a leopard in the sack is icing."

"So now what? The war is over. The world is at peace."

Mendoza walked back to the balcony, grabbed Ukweli by the hand, and gently led him back to the bed. "Then I guess you'll just have to conquer me again." He smiled and they shared an ardent embrace.

Ukweli sat at the head of the table in the offices of the Church of the Seer in midtown Atlanta. The spaces were exceptionally well kept, as established in the bylaws by Remington Cross. All rooms, including the bathrooms and the weapons depot, were spotless and the technology was updated every quarter. As Ukweli looked around the room at his team, he allowed himself a moment of pride. He genuinely loved these people and they loved him. They had been through so much together. Their losses had been great. Calvin and Marcus in Rome. Kelley in Venice. But given what they had experienced, it seemed nothing short of miraculous that they were still together in that room.

"The gala is next Saturday, January sixth, at an undisclosed location and is immediately followed by a reception at Prime Minister Walker's estate. If they planned on assassinating us, they probably wouldn't do it at the personal home of a public official, so I guess we're okay."

Adam sighed. "Man, the things you think about."

"I'm always thinking about the wellness and safety of my friends and family. This is the first official business trip where the sprouts and Kiera have been involved, so I'll assume nothing."

Paul spoke up. "I can admit I've really enjoyed the peace."

Ukweli said, "And I'm happy for you and Kei. I really am. But tell me that something about this whole ordeal doesn't give you the slightest pause."

Kei said, "Do you really think Alexander would do anything to hurt us?"

"Alexander wouldn't, but we know very little about who he's working for," Charlotte replied.

Paul added, "If you really think there might be danger, why are we going? Why are you taking your children?"

"Look, I want to believe that Alexander is who he says he is, so I'm giving him the benefit of the doubt. And even I can admit the peace is holding so far."

Adam said, "So what then? Are we going or not?"

Ukweli took a deep breath. "We're going, but don't let your guard down for a minute. I don't trust them until I do."

JANUARY 6, 2052

Ukweli was surprised to learn the gala was to take place at the Connaught Festivity Hall at Highgate School in London. Ukweli, Kiera, the sprouts, Adam, and Paul were all taken on a tour of the new facilities at Highgate, which included an indoor fast-flow pool for crew and distance swim training, a new state-of-the-art soccer simulator, and several new squash courts. The mixture of new technology with old-world architecture was a perfect representation of what made Highgate special. Ukweli and his friends felt like they had walked back in time, back to the 2030s when they had occupied those same hallways. They looked at old pictures and took new ones. Ukweli showed the sprouts the dojo where he and Paul had trained in the martial arts, and the chess room where he and Adam had competed.

Kiera experienced nostalgia that made her long for simpler times. She remembered walking the halls at Highgate with Ukweli . . . and Jackson, and it made her sad to know all of that had turned into all of this. She was thrilled with her children and she loved Ukweli dearly, but there was a lack of fulfillment that she fought, trying not to seem needy and selfish. She had loved Ukweli almost her whole life, and now she found herself wondering if there was more out there. She immediately felt guilty for those thoughts and reminded herself of her many blessings. She decided this trip would be about celebrating where she was. She would participate in honoring her husband and his team. She would share her past with her children. She would look forward to a peaceful future, if the stories were correct, where she would finally have the family she had always wanted. She knew Ukweli loved her. Didn't he?

None of the speeches were long, as the pre-gala cocktail hour had claimed more than a few victims. Ukweli, of course, remained fully sober, not just because he didn't drink, especially in front of strangers, but he simply couldn't let go of the feeling that something was out of place. He could admit he was honored by the presentations and the kind words from the World Society. If he wasn't such a naturally untrusting person, he might even have been impressed. He really enjoyed the songs by the children's choir. They hadn't had one when he was at Highgate. It wasn't as if he would've been in the choir. Ukweli wasn't a songbird. Uzuri was a great singer, though. She would've been a great choir member.

Ukweli's speech was short. He knew almost everyone in the audience was intoxicated and he didn't want to waste good words on a less-than-attentive crowd. He thanked the members of the World Society High Council for the honor. He thanked his team. He thanked his wife. He thanked his children. He honored Calvin, Marcus, and Kelley. He charged the High Council with honoring the treaty. He kissed his wife, who stood with him on stage. He lifted Kip into his arms. He gave Pax a pat on the head and he and his family walked backstage. Mrs. Bergstrom was there waiting on the children. Ukweli handed Kip back to Kiera, kneeled and gave Pax a big hug, and kissed Mrs. Bergstrom on the cheek.

"Well done, sir. I thought your speech was excellent." Mrs. Bergstrom was very encouraging.

"I agree. I'm glad you kept it short. These heels are higher than I want my heels to be right now."

"We're about to head to the prime minister's estate. Once those meetings are over, we'll head straight back to the hotel. You can take off the heels and the bra. Although, you are absolutely killing that dress. I mean, you look good in everything, but blue is your color."

"You said the same thing about the red dress I wore last month. And the green dress I wore in October."

"Well, I guess when you're Kiera Aseyori, all the colors are yours."

"You're such a flirt. I can't believe I ever fell for your nonsense." Kiera couldn't hide her smile.

"Nah, this is true. You are absolutely the most beautiful woman in the world."

"To you, maybe."

"Kiera, I'm positive that all those camera flashes were not for me. You'll be on the cover of magazines next week."

"Okay, okay, I am kinda fly." They laughed and kissed.

The Prime Minister of England was Dr. Richard Oliver Thomas "Tommie" Walker VI. Tommie's great-great-grandfather, Richard II, owned the large plantation, having grown wealthy from the cotton export in the 1880s. Tommie's grandfather, Richard IV, grew astronomically wealthy after inventing and patenting a superefficient motor for generators, still a major British export today. Tommie decided the best way for him to honor his legacy was to go into politics to manipulate the legislature. This was his chosen path to generational wealth. Nothing was more important to Tommie Walker than the Walker name. And since his abusive, alcoholic father had done everything he could to ruin it all, Tommie took even greater pride in restoring the name and protecting the fortune, so much so that the day before he left for college, he put maitotoxin in his father's whiskey and eagerly awaited word that he had perished from eating contaminated shellfish. His plan was executed flawlessly and no one ever suspected him. He carried that information alone and without a shred of regret.

The prime minister's estate was a sprawling three thousand acres surrounding a grand seventy-five-thousand-square-foot main home that featured fifteen bedrooms and twenty-two bathrooms. There was a basketball court, a bowling alley, a barbershop, a fully staffed medical wing with a pharmacy, three pools, two outdoor and one indoor, a helipad, and an airstrip. The nearby vineyards produced award-winning Pinot Noir and the truffles rooted out of the slightly alkaline soil in the oak forests were in high demand.

Tommie spent most of his days playing host to world leaders, earning their trust, providing them with every vice the world had to offer, capturing them in compromising situations, and blackmailing them to keep exports flowing out of London and resources flowing in. It was a highly effective system. In fact, Tommie learned that most leaders didn't even have to be coerced into behaving poorly. They enjoyed mischief and often traveled to London for the privilege.

Tommie was tall, handsome, well-connected, and wealthy. He ran in elite circles. Aside from other world leaders, his community included athletes, entertainers, and debutants from six continents. Tommie had never previously met Ukweli or any member of the Church of the Seer. But he knew them all. They had a reputation for toppling corrupt governments, so he worked hard to stay off their radar. Tonight, though, would provide a unique opportunity. Tommie would introduce Ukweli to one of his best friends. He had anticipated this meeting for months.

With the sprouts safe and sound with Mrs. Bergstrom at the hotel, Ukweli and Kiera, along with the other team members, arrived at the Walker estate. Everyone was impressed. The gathering was a collection of some of the world's most famous people, and no expense was spared.

Immediately upon climbing the great stairs and entering the massive front room, Ukweli was greeted by Alexander.

"There's the man of the hour. Welcome back to the UK, UK!" Ukweli smiled at Alexander's corniness.

"Hello, Alexander. This is all very impressive."

"Oh, you don't know the half. There is so much to see and hear. Hey, let me grab you a tonic water." Alexander summoned a serviceman, who quickly fetched a glass of tonic water over a perfectly clear sphere of ice. Alexander grabbed a glass of champagne and handed it to Kiera. "My, my, my, you are just the picture of perfection. Aphrodite must be green with jealousy. Simply angelic."

"You're too kind, Alexander. Thank you. How have you been?"

"Honestly, Kiera, I've never been better. I miss my Kelley something awful, but my mind is so clear and my purpose so defined. I'm embracing my passions, and it gives me life."

"I'm so happy for you. And you look great, by the way. Can I assume there is a young lady in your space?"

"You can, and you would be correct. In fact, she has changed everything for me. Not to put too strong a point on it, but she has been instrumental in freeing my mind. You know, you must dive into the pool of freedom headfirst."

"That's great. Perhaps we can all meet her soon."

"I have no doubt." Alexander smiled in a way that made Kiera happy for him. It made Ukweli uncomfortable. "Listen, Kiera, I need to borrow your husband for just the briefest of moments. There are more than a few people here who are excited to meet him. I'll have him back to you in a flash. I promise. If you need anything, please just say the word. These people are all here to honor you."

"Thank you, Alexander. I'll be fine."

Ukweli turned to Kiera. "Hey, don't stray too far from the guys. I'll be *back in a flash*." They kissed and he turned to follow Alexander's direction.

Alexander patted Ukweli on the back and led him up another set of stairs and into the library. The room was much too large to be a personal study, though there was a desk near the window. Alexander pointed to the sofa next to the fireplace and asked Ukweli to have a seat.

Ukweli asked, "So, what's going on? Which grubby politician am I meeting first?"

Alexander vigorously shook his head. "Oh no, Ukweli. The politicians are all downstairs indulging. Meet them at your leisure."

"Then who am I meeting now?"

Alexander put his hand on Ukweli's shoulder. "I want you to meet the special woman in my life."

"Oh, okay. That's cool. Should I go get Kiera?"

"No, no, sir. I want you to meet her first. She's such a big fan. She's really been looking forward to this."

At that time Tommie Walker entered the room with a woman walking behind him.

Alexander said, "Well look, there she is now."

Ukweli stood up and shook Tommie's hand. Tommie said, "Captain Aseyori, please meet the goddess Mithras."

The woman stepped out from behind Tommie and into the light. Ukweli quickly lifted his face and felt the blood rush to his head. He took two steps backward and almost tripped over the fireplace instruments.

Eyes wide open, he said, "That's impossible." He was amazed to be staring into the face of Camille Blanchet.

"Hello, Ukweli. It's good to see you again."

Ukweli squinted. "Camille?"

"Ahh, yes, my cameo in the Dragon dimension."

"Cameo? You deserve an Oscar."

"I was only there to observe."

"Why are you here?"

"Still mostly to observe, until the time is right to mobilize."

"Why are you watching me?"

"I'm monitoring your training."

"You must know I have no idea what you mean."

"Tell me, Captain Aseyori, how well do you know yourself?" The goddess slowly walked toward Ukweli.

"I'm always with me, so I would say pretty well." His tone balanced sarcasm with disbelief.

"Do you love your wife?"

"Of course."

Camille was close enough to touch his hand. "If you love your wife and you know yourself, why are you constantly in situations that betray her trust?"

"I never claimed to be perfect."

Alexander cleared his throat. "That's why you should be ever so grateful for the mercy of the goddess. Though you have fallen short, she has still chosen you."

"Chosen me for what?"

The goddess now held Ukweli's left hand sandwiched between hers. "Tell me what you know of your maternal grandmother."

"Nothing. She died before I was born, and my mother never spoke of her."

"Your grandmother didn't die. She was sacrificed."

"Sacrificed?"

"She gave her life to secure your future. Your father required it."

"My father? Kabeyesi?"

"See? You don't know who you are!"

"I don't understand." Ukweli was genuinely confused, and his expression didn't hide it.

"Kabeyesi is not your father."

Ukweli struggled to hide his bewilderment. He knew he had never truly felt a connection with Kobe, but he had never been given any reason to believe it was for anything other than personality clashes.

"Of course he is. Kobe Aseyori is my father. He raised me."

"You know in your heart that he is not. You've always known."

Ukweli's growing agitation caught the attention of Alexander and Yazata began to materialize. "Why should I believe a single thing you have to say?" The deep growl in his voice filled the room with tension.

"I'm only offering you truth, Ukweli." Her right hand moved to his forearm.

"Then who, *Camille*? Who is my father?"

Alexander grabbed Ukweli firmly by the bicep with a jerking motion. "You will address her as goddess."

Ukweli looked at Alexander's hand on his arm before fixing his gaze on his eyes. It was his first time noticing they were blue. "Brother, have you gone insane?"

The goddess touched both men on the shoulder. "Gentlemen, please do try to remain calm." She turned toward Alexander. "This is a lot for Ukweli to process. Please summon patience."

Ukweli didn't look away from Alexander. "You should listen to her, bruv." Alexander released his arm and took three small steps to the side and clasped his hands behind his back.

The goddess looked toward Alexander and then to Tommie. "Leave us." They calmly left the room. Yazata fully materialized in front of the large bay window overlooking the east fountains.

"Camille, please tell me what you know of my father, if you do indeed insist it's not Kobe."

"Ukweli, your maternal great-grandmother was born Ellie Moss. Her father was a working-class tradesman in London, and he bartered his soul for status to elevate in the growing movement known as the Craft of the Wise. Ellie grew up in the Craft and was eventually chosen to bear the line. In exchange for the honor, she pledged the life of her daughter, your grandmother, so that her granddaughter, your mother, could perpetuate the line."

"What line? My mother never spoke of any family lineage."

"Your grandmother gave her life so that you could rise, when it was time."

"Time for what?"

"Dominion. Ukweli, your father is Amon-Ra, the glorious god of the sun." The goddess placed her hand on Ukweli's face and he was shown visions of power and glory and world dominance. He saw himself sitting on a large golden throne that rested on the crown of the sun, and there were lions on either side of him singing praises. "This is your destiny, Ukweli. You have been created to rule the Earth with the power of the darkness at the center of the sun."

Suddenly, the sun in the vision became volatile and flaming winds began to stir. The lions were swept away and the sun exploded with a great flash of light. Ukweli fell down to earth and was suddenly returned to his present scene.

Yazata stepped back. "It is too soon. The light remains."

"It's not too soon. It's the Magician." Yazata began to blur and eventually faded. The goddess stepped toward Ukweli and lightly grasped both of his hands.

"Ukweli, listen to me. You have an incredible power, a power that can change the entire world. In fact, I fear that if you are unwilling to accept your responsibility, the world may be in danger. You alone can save it. Peace is fragile. It will need something, someone, to stabilize it. You are the only one who can. I can only hold things in place temporarily. You must accept your destiny." She gently pulled his face toward hers and kissed him. "Dominion, Ukweli. It is the only way."

Ukweli blinked and the goddess was gone.

As he gathered himself, Tommie and Alexander came into the room followed by two men carrying crystal tumblers and a decanter of premium scotch. They proposed a toast to the new lord of the land. Ukweli, still stunned and unstable, grabbed a glass and drank to his new future. Confused and unable to speak, he just swallowed and smiled as the visions continued to play in his mind.

"Power!" They drank.

"Glory!" They drank.

"Dominion!" They drank.

Ukweli tried to focus but couldn't seem to find his bearings. He looked at Alexander and said, "My family . . ."

"They're fine, Ukweli. We've already escorted them back to the hotel. You, sir, still have a big night ahead of you!" He lightly patted Ukweli on the chest and grinned as he spoke. The door opened and four beautiful women walked into the room and began to embrace and caress Ukweli.

Tommie smiled slyly. "Ahh, such are the spoils of the strong." He and Alexander followed the servants out of the room, leaving Ukweli and his concubines to their carnality.

Tommie Walker employed nearly one hundred servants at his estate. They performed all the duties in the maintenance of the grounds, including landscaping, plumbing and electrical, cleaning, and cooking in addition to maintaining his twenty automobiles, his mega yacht, his helicopter, and his private jet. Each member of his staff had to pass extensive physical and mental examinations and was strictly prohibited from discussing anything that took place at the Walker estate. His staff was loyal, partly because they were well paid—most of them made in excess of one hundred pounds per hour—and partly because they feared Tommie Walker. Several servants had died unexpectedly and mysteriously after posing questions about Tommie's business dealings.

Tommie also employed what he playfully called his League of Nerds—accountants, attorneys, physicians, and the like. They all had information that could likely incriminate him in one area or another. None of them would dare cross Tommie Walker, though.

It wasn't so much Tommie that they feared, but his number-one lieutenant, Sara Gamble. Sara executed all of Tommie's visions. She was the one who made things happen. The heads of each division reported to her. No one spent a dime without her knowledge. No one spoke a word without her hearing it. When things needed to be handled, Sara handled them. Anytime you saw Tommie, you could be sure Sara was never far behind.

It was Sara who approached Kiera in the great room at the Walker estate to inform her that Ukweli would be with

Tommie the remainder of the night and that she would be escorted back to the hotel.

"What do you mean, the rest of the night?" Kiera was indignant.

"I do certainly apologize for the inconvenience, but it seems Dr. Walker has much to discuss with your husband."

"Then I'll just grab a crab puff and wait here. Excuse me, garçon—"

Sara interrupted. "I'm sorry, but that isn't possible."

"Then tell me what is, because I'm not leaving without Ukweli."

"Please, Mrs. Aseyori, I understand, but I assure you the captain is in no danger. He is among friends. The World Society has big plans for him, and it is vital that they have a chance to brief him on his future."

"His future is my future."

"Mrs. Aseyori, your car is outside." Two large men approached and stood behind Sara. Kiera looked around, but none of the Seers were in view. She looked at the guards and decided perhaps this wasn't the best time for a confrontation. She reluctantly turned and walked out the front doors and down the steps. As she approached the car, the driver got out and opened the rear passenger door, allowing her to enter. Kiera was unaware Sara had followed her out.

Once she looked settled in the back seat, Sara leaned in to speak. "I do hope you have enjoyed your time with us. We'll take . . . good care of your husband." Sara smiled as she closed the door and turned to climb the stairs.

Kiera had an entire arsenal of choice words she wished she could unleash on Sara in that moment. She chose discretion. Kiera did not like choosing discretion. She fumed in silence the entire drive back to the hotel such that she was angrier when she arrived than when she had left the Walker estate. She walked into the hotel and went to the room where her children were being entertained by Mrs. Bergstrom.

"How have they been?" She was still fuming and aggressively removed her coat.

"Lovely as always. Kiera, dear, how about if I hold the children for the evening and you can go to your room and have a calming bath and relax your spirit."

"Thank you." Kiera kissed her children and ordered them to behave for Mrs. Bergstrom. She walked quickly to the penthouse suite, still upset. When she got to the door, she opened it and stormed through the room to the balcony. She wanted to scream but didn't want to disturb the neighbors, so she just cried. She sat on one of the chairs and cried. Kiera didn't like being embarrassed and she didn't like being told what to do.

Ukweli could've told me himself, she thought. And suddenly she found herself resenting him. She thought of the moment he came into her living room followed by a pregnant Mendoza. *He called her Claire. Uggh.* She began to imagine what debauchery he was probably involved in at the very moment. *He's never been faithful to me. Why do I put up with this?* The more she thought, the more she cried. She was startled when a hand touched her shoulder.

"It seems we always meet with your eyes full of tears."

Kiera quickly stood and turned to face the voice. "Brad? What are you doing here?"

"I'm in town for the banquet. I saw you on stage. You're so beautiful." He lightly touched the side of her face.

"No, I mean what are you doing here, in my room? How did you even get in here?"

"The concierge knows I'm a friend of your family. We both saw you come into the hotel in distress, so he was kind enough to give me a key card so I could check on you. I'm only here because I care."

"Thank you for caring, but I'm fine. Please see yourself out."

"Kiera, why do we continue to play these games?" Hassan moved closer to her.

"There are no games, Brad. Please leave."

"You know he doesn't deserve you. He has only brought stress and disappointment into your life. You can do better. You deserve better."

"That's not for you to decide. Please leave."

Hassan grabbed Kiera by the arm, gently at first, but she could feel him putting pressure on her forearm. "Come with me. Let me show you what real love is. Make love to me just once and I promise you'll forget about him. We can leave all of this behind." He forcibly pulled her from the balcony into the front room as he spoke.

"Don't do this, Brad. I'm asking you to leave. Please let me go!"

He threw her onto the couch and lay on top of her. He covered her mouth and began to grope her lower body. "You'll learn to love me as I love you."

"Please, Brad . . . no . . . please . . . Don't do this."

"I'm doing this for us, Kiera. You'll learn to love me."

Hassan felt pressure on the back of his head and heard a click. He stopped moving and put his hands on the couch.

Mrs. Bergstrom stood beside him holding a pistol to his head. "The lady has asked you to leave."

Hassan slowly pushed himself off the couch and stood in front of Mrs. Bergstrom. "You don't know who you're messing with. This is way above your pay grade, old lady."

"I'm sure it is. Run along now." She motioned toward the door with her gun.

Hassan started toward the door but quickly turned. "Kiera, you're far too trusting and very misguided."

"Please walk while you talk, sir." Mrs. Bergstrom looked comfortable holding the pistol. Hassan could tell it wasn't her first time.

He reluctantly turned back to the door. "Kiera, do you know where Ukweli is right now? Do you know what he's doing right now?"

Kiera sat up. "Get out, Brad. Get out now."

"Kiera, he's been lying to you all this time. Do you even know who Dakota Williams really is? Do you? How about Bryce James? Do you know who he is?"

Kiera stood and pointed toward the door. "Please leave, Brad."

"I'm going, Kiera. But you must get your head out of the sand. Ukweli doesn't love you. He never has and he never will. You're trying to build a future with someone who is toxic and volatile. He is nothing but quicksand. You have no idea the darkness that lives in him. I can only hope you will come to your senses before it's too late." He quickly turned and walked out of the door.

Kiera looked up at Mrs. Bergstrom with puzzled gratitude. "Too late for what?" Mrs. Bergstrom sat beside her and Kiera cried on her shoulder.

"Our efforts to corrupt the light have, once again, proven ineffective."

"The plant grew impatient. He may have jeopardized the mission. Elimination may be our only option."

"Then the man should do it."

"Yes, I agree. It should be the man."

Ukweli woke up the following morning in a very large bedroom with the sunlight pouring through the window and crashing on his face. It was bright and he had to squint, but it felt warm on his skin and made him smile. He felt empowered. He took a deep breath and tried to lift his arms to stretch. That's when he realized he wasn't alone. He slowly pulled back the bamboo viscose comforter to reveal four women, all nude, asleep in the bed with him. He tried to think back to remember what had happened, but the visions seemed more a dream than reality and he couldn't believe he could spend a night with four women and not remember it. Ukweli was startled when he heard Tommie's voice on the other side of the room.

"Good morning, Ukweli. I see you had a great night. I must say, I do admire your stamina. They are all sleeping like babies." Tommie showed his teeth as he sat in the large chair with his legs crossed.

Ukweli sat up on his elbows. "Tommie, what the hell is going on?"

"I'm here to retrieve your concubines and to pass on some excellent news." Tommie walked to the bed and clapped a few times. "Okay, ladies, let's go. Good show, job well done. Well done indeed." The women moved slowly at first but then with great haste as they dressed and left the room.

"Tommie, please."

"Ukweli, you'll never believe the surprise I have for you this morning." Tommie clapped again and the door opened. Two of the servants entered the room holding Hassan by either arm. They escorted him to the chair at the foot of the bed and sat him down with a thud.

Ukweli got out of bed and grabbed the robe off the floor. "Hassan? What's going on?"

"Ukweli, don't believe anything they tell you!" Ukweli could tell Hassan was under a great deal of stress.

Tommie giggled. "Well, you see, Ukweli, it seems Brad Hassan assaulted your lovely wife last night."

"What?" Ukweli shouted.

"That's not true! I was only following orders! I didn't—" One of the servants put tape over his mouth. They also bound his arms to the chair.

Tommie continued, "Well, as it turns out, Hassan has had an affinity for your wife for some time now. He saw an opportunity last night. He went to your hotel room and made his move. I've been told he was pretty aggressive."

"You would disrespect my family this way?" Ukweli's head was slightly tilted.

Hassan vigorously shook his head no. Tommie could see the fury growing deep inside Ukweli. He reached into his coat pocket and pulled out a pistol with a silencer. He stood and calmly offered it to Ukweli.

"You know what you have to do."

"What?"

"This man has violated your wife. You trusted him with your son, and this is how he repays you? You've known all along that he was up to no good. If you allow him to walk out of here right now, he'll know forever he did the most dastardly of deeds and you didn't respond. You simply cannot allow it."

"Why, Hassan? Why would you do this? Do you see the position you've put me in?"

Hassan's voice was muffled by the tape. He continued to shake his head. Tommie retrieved a device from his lapel pocket. "Ahh, I didn't want to put you through this, Captain, but it seems you need a push toward justice." After pressing a series of buttons, a sound began to play. Ukweli immediately recognized Kiera's voice.

"Don't do this, Brad. I'm asking you to leave. Please let me go!"

"You'll learn to love me as I love you."

"Please, Brad . . . no . . . please . . . Don't do this."

"I'm doing this for us, Kiera. You'll learn to love me."

Ukweli recalled his interactions with Hassan in the past. He remembered Kiera licking the ice cream cone after she got out of his car. The more he thought, the more his resolve grew. He calmly grabbed the gun from Tommie's hand.

"You know, I told Kiera what would happen to you if you ever touched her." With no further hesitation, he put two bullets into Hassan's chest and one into his head . . . and it felt good. Ukweli had taken life before, but never like this. This was the most satisfying kill he had ever known. Even watching the life leave Vasher's face didn't compare. Ukweli felt powerful. He was in charge. He felt like a king. He had almost allowed himself to forget how good it felt to take life. Suddenly his visions became clear. He saw himself sitting at the top of the sun receiving praise. He had a vivid recollection of his excursion from the night before. He saw himself being worshipped by the concubines, and it felt good. He was strong. He was dangerous. He was the son of a god. He now knew how it felt to have cosmic power. He looked at Tommie and said, "You know, Tommie, some people just have to learn the hard way."

Tommie smiled. "Captain, I couldn't agree more." Servants entered the room and began to clear the scene.

When Ukweli arrived at the hotel, he found Kiera with the sprouts and Mrs. Bergstrom enjoying breakfast. They were spoiling themselves with sweet delectables, and each plate had omelets and crab claws. The irony wasn't lost on him. He walked into the room and went to the sprouts first. He kissed Kip on the cheek and Pax on the forehead. He hugged Mrs. Bergstrom from behind and kissed her cheek. He walked to Kiera and said, "Hey, can I talk to you for a moment?"

Kiera finished chewing a bite of waffle. "Of course."

They walked to the bedroom and closed the door. Kiera sat on the side of the bed. Ukweli sat in a chair.

"Kiera, listen, about last night."

"Oh, I know, Tommie's thug told me you would be with him all night."

"No, not that. I'm talking about Hassan."

Kiera blushed. "How do you know about that?"

"Kiera . . ."

"Ukweli, it was nothing. I think he had been drinking."

"What do you mean, nothing? And being drunk is no excuse for assaulting you."

"Assaulting me? Wait, I wouldn't say he assaulted me. Nothing happened between Brad and me. Why would you say something like that?"

"You mean . . ."

"Ukweli, Brad was a little aggressive, but Mrs. Bergstrom came in and he left. Still, how do you know about that?"

"Well, that's not important. I'm so sorry I wasn't here to protect you. I'll never leave you that vulnerable again. You mean the world to me. I love you with all my heart."

"I love you, too, UK." Ukweli's sudden tenderness concerned Kiera. "Hey, are you all right?"

"Kiera, babe, I've never had greater clarity for my life and our future. I just can't wait to get started."

"Get started with what?"

"Dominion."

His expression made her uncomfortable and reminded her of Jackson's language just before he had gone off the deep end. But she had seen darkness in Ukweli before, and she convinced herself this time was no different than the others. They went back to the front room and finished breakfast as a family before boarding the jet and returning to Zurich. On the flight home, Ukweli casually mentioned to Kiera that they would need to find a new soccer coach for Pax. Kiera thought it was an overreaction, but he insisted and she eventually agreed. Pax didn't seem to care, but thought it odd that Coach Hassan would leave for another assignment in the middle of the season.

"The man is returning home with the light. Minimally compromised."

"We must expedite the process."

"He needs activity, but he must believe it to be for grand and noble purposes."

"We must also reactivate the siren and increase the flow of concubines."

"Only months remain until the lunar event."

"Yes, mobilize the purdah."

13

THE RETURN TO THE SWORD

MARCH 22, 2052

Ukweli sat in the basement in Zurich staring at the computer screens as the Church of the Seer logos spun around on each display. He had become something of a world star overnight following the banquet recognition and his face had appeared on magazine covers. It was important to the World Society that all nations recognized the activities of the Church of the Seer, Ukweli in particular, and the role they played in keeping the world safe during the turbulent times when Imperium was in charge. Ukweli had defeated the Dragon, killed Vasher, and decimated the forces of evil until they ran and hid in the hills. So Ukweli now served the World Society in a humanitarian role. He didn't have any real responsibilities, but he allowed them to use his name, image, and likeness in their Campaigns of Peace all over the world so that his face became synonymous with freedom and prosperity. Of course, this freedom was maintained by a small, select group of influential individuals who made sure the charismatic leaders had more than enough while they, in turn, convinced those who had almost nothing that their progression up to very little was only the beginning of their journey to wealth and relevance. Ukweli represented hope to the world. He was more popular than he had been as a young soccer phenom in London. It became more and more difficult for him to honor his marriage vows. So many desirable opportunities. He was bound to break soon.

Ukweli waited at the desk for a phone call from President James. They didn't let him know the nature of the call ahead of time, so he was slightly eager and a little anxious. He hoped this would be the first of a set of real activities. He enjoyed the benefits of fame, but he was getting tired of having nothing to do. He loved Kiera and he adored the sprouts, but maybe Mendoza was right. Perhaps he wasn't meant to be a stay-at-home dad. He needed something to conquer.

Ukweli was excited to see the shimmering red phone icon appear and was slightly surprised to see President James had shaved his beard.

"Good afternoon, Captain. Thank you for making time."

"Good afternoon, sir. I like the new look. It's clean."

"Well, my wife loves it, but my girlfriend hates it. But you know what they say, happy wife, blah blah." He shrugged.

Ukweli chuckled. "What can I do for you, sir?"

"Captain, we have been investigating a new threat, and we need your expertise."

"What kind of threat, sir?"

"Our research has indicated there are pockets of torqueo anima active here in the States."

"Torqs? That's impossible . . . or at least unlikely, sir."

"We thought so too. But one of our operatives responded to a disturbance in Atlanta."

"Those are rare these days. I'm surprised Charlotte didn't hear about it."

"They're extremely rare. That's why we decided to look into it."

"And your operatives found torqs?"

"They were met with what they described as large figures with extraordinary strength and skill with slightly disfigured features. They engaged and we lost two of our best men. The survivors reported hearing high-pitched shrieking noises during the fierce fighting. Honestly, they were fortunate to escape."

"Torqs don't organize themselves. There has to be someone behind it."

"Exactly. That's why we think Imperium may still have boots on the ground. If they are allowed to reorganize, they pose a threat to everything the World Society has accomplished."

"That's insane. I was sure we completely eradicated them. Should I reassemble my team?"

"No, Captain. We want you to personally handle this assignment. The fewer people who know about this, the better."

"That's against protocol. The Church of the Seer operates in units. Even if I'm on a solo mission, there is always someone monitoring my movements. Not to mention the disposal crew. That's not how I'm accustomed to working."

"Then you'll just have to adjust. You're not working for the Church of the Seer any longer. You represent the World Society now. We need this done quickly and discreetly. You're the only person with the skill and expertise to get this done. Are you up to it?"

"Of course, sir. I'll take care of it."

"I knew I could count on you. You know, Captain, of all the people who exist in the world, you're the only one who can do what you do. That must feel pretty good."

"Well, let's see what happens in Atlanta. I'll get back to you." Ukweli smiled. The call ended.

Just as the screens went black, Kiera opened the basement door and walked down the stairs. Ukweli stayed in his chair but turned to face her.

"Hey, babe." He reached for her, inviting her to sit in his lap. She smiled and sat across his lap with an arm around his shoulders.

"How was your call with the president?"

"Curious. He's sending me to Atlanta. He says they found torqs there."

"Torqs? I thought you said the war with Imperium was over."

"I was sure it was. Charlotte maintains a twenty-four-hour scan for torqs and she hasn't heard anything."

"Then why does he think torqs are there?"

"Some of their guys fought a group of them. The description fits."

"I didn't think the World Society had a military wing."

"Me either. But if there are torqs organized, it represents a bigger problem."

"So, are you calling your team in?"

"No, they've asked me to handle this alone. They're prioritizing discretion."

"So why are you telling me?"

"You're my wife and you deserve to know why I'm leaving."

Kiera kissed him and said, "You're my husband and you deserve to know they're setting you up."

"What do you mean?"

She kissed him again. "The only reason they're dragging you back into this is to use you as a martyr."

"That's not true, Kiera. President James said himself that I'm the only person capable and qualified to complete this mission."

She kissed him a third time. "President James is a master manipulator. You told me that."

"Hey, quit kissing me just to help your argument."

"I'm kissing you because I love kissing you. Besides, if you're going to allow yourself to be a lackey for President James, I may not be able to kiss you much longer."

"That's morbid."

"That's honesty."

"You know I have to do this, so please just be supportive."

"I love you and I support you. So much, in fact, that while you reopen a lifelong war with the possible remnant of Imperium, I'll be here raising your children like a good little housewife. So please don't question my commitment. This affects me as much as it does you."

"That's why I told you." They kissed again and their passion kindled.

Ukweli arrived at the Church of the Seer headquarters in Atlanta and was surprised to be greeted by a familiar voice over the comms.

"Good morning, Captain."

"Claire? What are you doing here?"

"I was assigned to this mission by the World Society. They sent me here to monitor your activity. I'll meet you in the weapons depot. They gave me your briefing packet."

She hurried to the elevator in hopes that she could beat him downstairs. Mendoza loved few things more than watching Ukweli enter a room. She watched him walk around the corner down the last few stairs. This man still made her heart skip a beat. After all this time. After all she knew. She loved him more now than she ever had.

She walked over to meet him and gave him a hug with her right hand. She held the communicator in her left hand, which she gave to Ukweli. "The information you'll need is on here. I looked it over, but I don't understand torq behavior like you do, so some of it didn't make sense to me."

"I'll figure it out. We'll have to stay off the comms, though."

"I know."

"Does the report say how many there are?"

"Eight at last count."

"Do we know where they are?"

"They're gathered at the abandoned Christ the King cathedral."

"That's where Incursus was killed. That must've been ten years ago."

"Eleven . . . almost to the day."

"Hey, if you're here, where is Gabby? I'm gonna be furious if you say she's with PT."

"I left her with the one person who seems to love her as much as I do."

"You came here and left Gabby in Zurich?"

"You left Pax and Kip. Why is that any different?"

"I left Pax and Kip with their *mother*."

"Honestly, UK, is there anyone you trust Gabby with more than Kiera?"

"No."

"Me either. So, focus and let's get this done. I need you back here as soon as possible."

Ukweli looked around the weapons cage and strangely decided to leave the guns there. He didn't grab armor either. He grabbed a simple black trench and strapped his swords to his back over the coat.

Mendoza looked confused. "You're not taking your guns?"

Ukweli answered without looking up. "No. I won't need them."

"And no armor?"

"No. I can't explain it, but it will only get in the way."

"Your swords are outside your coat. You'll have to fight—"

"Claire. I'll be fine."

Ukweli stepped out of the weapons cage and looked at Mendoza. She wore a black jumpsuit with her hair pulled back. A vigorous lust ignited between them. As he started walking toward her, she started running toward him. She jumped into his arms and they embraced.

"I've missed you, Claire." They kissed.

"I know. I've missed you, too, baby. Please hurry back."

Ukweli lifted his leg over his motorcycle and brought it to balance before lifting the kickstand with his heel and slowly rotating the accelerator handle. He remembered his first mission for the Church of the Seer, navigating the streets of Atlanta, then on a Damon Hyperspace, now on the upgraded Damon Premiere Mach Three, in silence as the powerful two-hundred-twenty-five-horsepower electric engine surged him through the streets well over the speed limits. It was a familiar feeling, and he could hardly contain his growing excitement. It had been over a year since he killed Vasher, but he had never stopped training. When you've taken as many lives as required by the Church of the Seer, you assume that someday the tables will turn and death will come looking for you. Ukweli figured he needed to stay ready. Death would have to bring its A-game to the fight. Ukweli had promised himself he would never go quietly. More importantly, he had a lot to lose if he were ever caught off guard. It paid to stay ready.

As he approached the cathedral he was saddened by the state of the building. A once glorious tribute to the glory of the god of the Vatican and the throne of Saint Peter, it now stood an ominous dark tower. The once vibrant stained-glass windows had long been boarded up. The construction was solid and the building looked strong, but uninviting. It was hard to believe that a beautiful wedding or an inspirational mass had ever taken place there. The gloom made it look more like a mausoleum. An image of Gargamel's house came to Ukweli's mind. He smiled. He drove right up to the front door and noticed movement on the corners.

Well, they know I'm here, he thought.

Ukweli climbed the few stairs from the front driveway to the large wooden doors. He tried to listen for movement inside, but before he could get his ear to the door, it opened. A small, quiet voice called to him from inside. It was the voice of a child.

"Captain Aseyori, please come inside."

Ukweli had seen a lot of things and wasn't afraid very often, but the sound of a beckoning child in this environment genuinely made his skin crawl.

"Dammit, that's creepy—even to me."

Ukweli slowly pulled the door the rest of the way open

and walked through the short vestibule before entering the main sanctuary. The high-arched ceilings and the tiled floor created an echo as he walked. The room wasn't completely dark, as light from three candles at the front of the room provided a sinister orange glow. Ukweli walked slowly and deliberately until he heard the voice again.

"Captain Aseyori, welcome."

Ukweli squinted a bit, but as he got closer to the light source, he could see that a girl in a light-blue dress was holding the center candle. As he approached the light, he was able to make out a face—a familiar face.

"DuaTre?"

"It's good to see you again, Captain."

"What on earth are you doing here? And why are you still in this form?"

"I'm afraid we don't have much time, Captain."

"What's going on?"

"It seems someone wants you dead."

"Yeah, what's new?"

"Someone powerful enough to resurrect the Torqueo Anima project."

"Someone wants to bring war back into the world."

"Your death will serve as a capable catalyst."

"They sent you to kill me?"

"I'm only here to configure the torqueo anima. It seems the new and improved machines respond to telepathy. Necromancers all over the globe have been mobilized and handsomely compensated."

"New and improved? Compensated by who?"

Before DuaTre responded, Ukweli could see a perplexed look on her face. She stepped closer to him and lifted her candle to his face. She looked deeply into his eyes. Ukweli straightened his posture.

"You have . . . awareness." Ukweli didn't respond. "You know of your diabolical heritage." She paused. "I see why they want you dead."

"What does that mean?"

"God or death. Either way, they win. Absolutely brilliant." DuaTre leaned back and laughed a loud, hearty laugh. "Good luck, Nigerian. Your foes are formidable, but you already knew that. If we don't meet again, please kiss your father for me. Given your sins, I seriously doubt you will join your mother in Caelum."

As she continued to laugh, the recessed lights in the wooden panels around the upper edge of the cathedral began to glow. Ukweli turned to see the forms of more than twenty large men scattered around the room. They moved in unison toward him. It was then that it happened.

Ukweli felt a rage inside like a ball of fire in his gut. It was painful at first and he knelt to keep from falling over. As the fire burned hotter in his belly, sharp pain radiated to his extremities and he let out a piercing scream. Suddenly, he felt warm and powerful. He stood and opened his eyes. He could see in the room as though it were lit by the midday sun. He gazed into the approaching torqs, and he could see beyond their mortal bodies into the forms of the demons who inhabited the machines.

The torqs spoke at once as with a single voice. "It is our pleasure to escort you to Baratrum."

Ukweli drew his sword and lunged at the first demon, striking him through the chest. He quickly turned and struck another in the neck before spinning and lowering his body to strike another in the abdomen. He moved with precision over and under pews, into and out of the aisles. He leaped from the floor to the walls and pushed off, giving his blade greater momentum. The shrieks of the fleeing demons were a symphony in the ears of the slayer as he moved with greater force and ferocity than he had ever known. The power provided a pleasure that infected Ukweli's senses so that even the smells, and yes, the tastes, of the destruction in his wake contributed to his glee. The edge of his blade was like a razor, and it sliced through flesh and bone like piranha teeth.

By the time Ukweli stopped to take a breath, there were twenty-seven machines lying dead in the sanctuary, covering the abandoned holy space with unimaginable mayhem. Ukweli replaced his sword and calmly walked out the front door.

When he returned to the facility, he went immediately to the showers, where he found an eager Mendoza waiting for him.

"Congratulations on another successful mission, Captain. The world truly owes you a debt."

"There were more torqs than we thought."

"You handled it."

"The intel lacked accuracy. I'm not used to working like this. The Church is efficient. The Society . . ."

"The Society is new. They don't know what they don't know. That's why you're so important. They need you." Mendoza looked Ukweli up and down and began to smile. "Now get in the shower, because I need you too."

14

DAKOTA'S BIRTHDAY PARTY

JULY 20, 2052

Kiera, with Pax and Kip in tow, made the forty-minute drive from Zurich to Waldi to attend Dakota's ninth birthday party. Pax didn't care much for parties, but he hadn't been very social since Coach Hassan left his soccer program. He continued to train on his own but, though he didn't care to admit it, he missed his friends. This party would give him a chance to reconnect, and he allowed himself to enjoy the anticipation. Kip liked Dakota and sincerely appreciated this opportunity to continue to develop her princess motif in the presence of actual subjects. She planned to ignore protocol and demand the first slice of cake. She was sure she would get it. Dakota would realize she was in charge and he would, in turn, fear her appropriately. It was a master plan.

Conny-Land was everything Pax hoped it would be—an ocean of distractions to relieve him from all of his current anxieties. He was concerned about his parents. His dad was gone more often and for longer periods of time, and his mom was drinking more and seemed sad even more than usual. The only thing that made her smile these days was Gabby.

Pax also didn't spend a lot of time around Kip. She was practically being raised by Mrs. Bergstrom. Most days, he would check on his mom and Kip before returning to the solitude of study or training. Gabby needed Kiera and Kiera needed Gabby. Kip needed Mrs. Bergstrom. Pax didn't need anybody. That was good because he didn't have anybody. No one cared, and Pax convinced himself he was okay with that.

Pax's main concern, though, was the dreams. They had started a few months back and caused sleepless nights. There was variety in the content, but they all ended the same. He always saw himself reaching for his father as he was falling into a lava pit. Pax always tried to save him, but he never could, and he would wake up in sweats with his heart beating rapidly from the trauma. He didn't know what the dreams meant, maybe they didn't mean anything at all, so he handled it the way he handled everything. He internalized it, tucked it away, and never spoke of it. Ukweli had taught him that stress and anxiety were just markers that you hadn't trained enough, so that's what he did. Pax trained. He worked on soccer skills and martial arts. He studied astrophysics and calculus. He focused on languages, and he even started making progress on the guitar. Then there was the coin. The time travel. The dilations. Six seconds.

Pax teamed up with Bryce and Dakota with the intention of visiting every park feature: the batting cages, the roller coasters, and the games. He wanted to eat park food, to a limited extent of course. He wanted to have fun with his friends. He noticed, however, that his friends were keeping a distance. They whispered behind his back. Pax wanted answers.

"Hey, what's going on?"

"What do you mean, Pax?" Bryce looked away as he spoke. Pax knew sarcasm when he heard it. His mom spoke to his dad like that all the time.

"Why are you guys acting funny?" Pax was genuinely concerned.

"They told us it was your fault." Dakota looked down, almost like he was embarrassed to share the news.

"What's my fault?"

"My mom said it was your fault that Coach Hassan had to leave. She said you're the reason we don't have a team anymore." Dakota kept looking down.

"I didn't have anything to do with that."

Bryce chuckled. "Yeah, but maybe your mom—" He was interrupted by Dakota's sharp elbow nudging his ribcage.

"What about my mom?" Pax unconsciously balled his fists as his curiosity morphed into offense.

Bryce chuckled again. "My mom said Coach Hassan had to leave because your mom was all over—"

Pax didn't wait to hear what his mom was *all over*. Before Bryce could get the next word out, Pax punched him in the chin, the stomach, and the inside of his knees. As Bryce collapsed to the ground, Pax jumped on top of him and began to choke him. Bryce tried to fight back but was no match for Pax in his rage. It was only when he heard Dakota yelling at him to stop that Pax looked around and realized he was completely out of control. He had given in to lesser urges to the point that he barely remembered why he was choking Bryce. Ashamed, he could hear Dakota running to get adult help. He quickly reached into his pocket, grabbed his coin, and flipped it high into the air. He could still sense the distortion with his eyes closed, and when he opened them, he was standing in front of his friends.

"They told us it was your fault."

"Huh?"

"Our moms, they said it was your fault that Coach Hassan had to leave."

"Oh, right. Well, I hope that wasn't the case, but I guess we'll have to find somewhere else to play. You guys have any ideas?"

As Dakota and Bryce talked about the other clubs in Zurich and whether they thought there were other good fits in the city, Pax could only think of one thing. *That was definitely more than six seconds.*

"His abilities are expanding."

"It's time. Bring them in."

15

HELIOPOLIS

Ukweli's dreams were intense. He frequently woke in the middle of the night with sweats and tremors. Kiera often slept on the futon in her closet because he became aggressively animated during his sleep and she was unable to wake him without risking physical harm. His visions were clear, though. He always remembered his dreams when he woke up because they were all the same. He was standing at the base of the staircase in his childhood home in Lagos. He watched his baby sister, Uzuri, walk down the stairs as he tried to stop her, with no avail. He would then be whisked away through the stars and dropped into a memory of him killing a potential torq based on algorithm data. He was taken to Rome and he watched his former teammates Marcus and Calvin die on the steps of the Vatican. He was suddenly in Venice just as Vasher was pulling the trigger with his barrel only a few inches from Kelley's face. Then to a dark room that turned into a bright throne room, where he was escorted to the top of a high mountain and placed on the throne while kings bowed at his feet. Suddenly, the throne was at the top of the sun, guarded by lions as the world sang praises. His dreams always ended the same way. There was a voice, a deep voice that said, *Come to me and take your place.*

Ukweli sat in the basement at his family home in Zurich and combed through his books on symbolism and dreams. He knew his dreams depicted real events but were from a perspective he hadn't lived, so they weren't his actual memories, but rather simulations. Ukweli searched for the meaning in the dreams to prompt them to stop. The more he searched, the more frustrated he became. He knew he had regrets; he didn't need dreams to tell him that. But the dreams never ended with the regrets. There were always visions of the holy throne, followed by the instructions.

As Ukweli searched with his face down, his skin began to crawl and he felt the pulse associated with the change in pressure. He was sensing. He closed his eyes and allowed himself to feel the creature in the room. It was about twenty feet away, but it was moving toward him. It seemed to carry the same structure as Yazata, but with far less chaos and greater gravitas. It was a spirit of royalty. It also carried a heaviness, a darkness that demanded attention. It connected to the darkness in Ukweli and opened his eyes. Ukweli recognized he wasn't in control, but he didn't feel threatened. The darkness in him welcomed the connection and the light in him didn't fight because it didn't sense danger. It was the warmest, most sinister greeting he had ever experienced.

With his eyes now open, he could see the pulsating light of the large being. The light was pure white, blinding white light that made Ukweli's eyes burn and water. The being spoke into his spirit.

Come. Your father waits for you. Your father waits for your son. Come.

Ukweli, knowing Kiera wouldn't approve of his travel plans with Pax, told her he was taking him to visit professional soccer training grounds. Kiera was glad to see him spending time with Pax. He had been away for months killing demons on behalf of the World Society, so she didn't question it. Pax thought it odd but knew his father, transient as he had become, would not put him in harm's way. So, the two of them flew to Egypt. Pax looked forward to touring the training grounds of Al Ahly Sporting Club, Egypt's most popular soccer team. Ukweli looked forward to meeting his father, the sun god Ra.

Ukweli stepped off the plane in Cairo and the warm dry air against his face felt familiar. The Church ran missions in Port Said and Ismailia, along the canal, but Ukweli had never gone into Cairo, generally choosing the military site at Kibrit instead. So, the familiarity he felt in Cairo wasn't due to a physical connection to the land. He just sensed he was home.

He had never traveled to the Middle East alone. He would've requested that Adam accompany him on this trip, except that his reason for being in Cairo was incredibly personal. He was looking for his father. He was very resourceful and had connections in every corner of the planet, but how was he supposed to explain to anyone who asked that the long-lost father he sought was the sun god, and that he had been informed of his origin story by a goddess he originally met in the Dragon dimension? He decided this was best deemed a solo mission.

The being in his home had led him to Egypt. His research had led him to Cairo. Ukweli found that the sun god Amon-Ra was known as Jupiter by the Romans and Zeus by the Greeks. Ukweli's mother had been born in Tanzania and the cults there called him Munga Jua, but Camille had only mentioned the name Ra, so Ukweli thought it prudent to begin his search in the desert. Seeking to travel discreetly, he and Pax flew commercially into Cairo and drove a rented vehicle south to Luxor.

Ukweli didn't know what to expect. He didn't know what he was looking for and had no idea what he might find, but he had been drawn to the temple complex so he assumed his efforts would at least be rewarded with more prudent questions. If Camille was right, this all belonged to him anyway.

The temple district was crowded with tourists, as expected, and Ukweli watched closely as he maneuvered through the paths. He kept Pax in front of him and guided him by his shoulder. Pax loved seeing new places and experiencing new things, but his father's hand on his shoulder was reassuring.

Ukweli's training accounted for his awareness in public settings, but without his team watching his back and tracking his steps, and with Pax walking in front of him, his senses were heightened and he noticed everything—the colors of the fabric on the outside of the makeshift tents, the contrasting scents of kofta and animal slaughter pits, the sound of the grains of sand dancing on the dry winds singing background for a man playing a lute. Ukweli had been born in Africa, a proud son of Nigeria, but Cairo seemed to be as different from Lagos as Atlanta, so he was extra careful as he navigated his new surroundings.

They walked along the Nile corridor and admired the

beauty of the merchant ships sailing through to different points in the city. It reminded Ukweli of his time in Islington, watching the boats in the canal. He was taken back to a simpler time, before the fame, and it made him miss his mother. He thought of the first time he saw Kiera in the park as a teenager, and he missed her too.

Ukweli spoke softly to Pax. "You know, I used to go to the canal in Islington and watch the boats. That's where I met your mom." Pax had indeed heard the story before, but he never grew tired of it. He smiled to think that there were days when his parents had actually liked each other.

They sat by the water until the sun began to fade. Ukweli listened as Pax explained the positioning of the stars over the Egyptian sky, and he realized how bright his son really was. He knew Pax was accelerated in his learning, but he sat amazed at the true depth of his knowledge. He marveled while Pax went on and on about astrophysics and philosophy and advanced mathematics. *I guess the kid knows more than soccer*, he thought. This was one of the rare moments in his life that Ukweli found himself just being a proud dad. That's why he also found it no coincidence that it was in this moment he began sensing. Ukweli motioned for Pax to come to him. He sat him between his legs and told him to close his eyes. Ukweli looked around, but he didn't see anything. Again, he felt the pressure and the hair on his arms and legs began to sway. He took a deep breath and listened. *Come.*

He opened his eyes and tapped Pax on the shoulders. "Let's go."

"Where are we going?"

"Northeast."

Ukweli drove, with Pax riding shotgun, northeast to the suburb of Heliopolis. They arrived at a small temple just off the main road. It looked like a site a tourist might visit, though there were no tourists around. It was covered in ancient hieroglyphics, and the stairs to the entrance led down into an open-air green area.

Pax was intrigued but concerned. "Where are we?"

"I'm not sure exactly, but we are meeting a very important person here."

"Who are we meeting, Dad?"

Suddenly, a booming voice projected from behind them. "So, this is my grandson, the soccer star!"

Ukweli and Pax both turned quickly at the sound of the voice. It was simultaneously strong and gentle, like a grandfather might be. The voice came from a tall, muscular man approaching from the darkest corner of the space. He was dressed in modern modesty. He wore blue jeans and a white hooded jacket with white sneakers. He had brown skin and a perfectly manicured gray beard. Ukweli was apprehensive but felt the presence of a kindred spirit. He was connected to this man in ways he couldn't explain. Pax felt no such connection. Ukweli pulled Pax closer to him.

"Who are you?"

"Ahh, Ukweli, must we continue with the acts? Come. Come and hug your father."

Ukweli released Pax and walked to the man and embraced him. In that moment, Ukweli was taken into his visions of regret and despair and saw them all wiped away, leaving only a clear sky full of stars. He began to weep as he lay in the arms of the man who held him as his very own.

"Father, how? How is this possible?"

"Your mother was a remarkable woman. She sacrificed a great deal for you to be here now."

"I have so many questions."

"We have very little time, so please choose your questions wisely."

"Why am I only now learning of you?"

"It is now that you need to know of me. Your time has come to impact this world."

"You are a god, and I am only a man. What impact can I have?"

"Your world is reaching a crossroads. It is not the first time your world has been on the brink of disaster, but it is the closest it has ever come to complete destruction."

"What can I do?"

"You have all you need to save your world—with one exception. You have the power and the passion. What you lack is Ma'at."

"I don't understand."

"She would laugh at your lack of understanding. Ma'at is the goddess of order and harmony. She is the goddess of balance. You will need her in order to save your world."

"How? How can I access Ma'at?"

"She is here with us now."

Out of the shadows emerged a beautiful figure. Ukweli recognized her immediately. It was Camille Blanchet.

"Hello, Ukweli."

"This is impossible. How is it that—"

Camille interrupted. "Ukweli, where is your faith? Remember, dominion is the only way. I'm here to ensure you can save your world." She walked toward Ukweli and kissed him. "We can do it, but we must do it together." She kissed him again. "You can't do it without me." She smiled and kissed him a third time, then she stepped away. The goddess looked toward the sun god. "He's not ready."

The sun god replied, "Then let's proceed with the trials. He'll respond." He approached Ukweli and touched his forearm. "Son, listen. The goddess brings structure to your passion and power. Without her, your world will certainly be destroyed. But you will need to appease her to ensure her participation. That is why my grandson is so important."

"Wait, what does any of this have to do with Pax?"

The man laughed so heartily he leaned back. Images of Santa Claus came into Ukweli's mind.

"What does this have to do with Pax, you ask? Ukweli, this is *all* about Pax! It is only the potential of his worthiness that makes this transaction possible."

"'Potential of his worthiness'?"

"Pax must still prove he is worthy of the honor of perpetuating the royal line. If he is found worthy, the goddess will bond with you so you can save your world. If, however, he proves to be unworthy, the goddess will reject him. You, and your world, and everything you know and love, will be destroyed. The goddess will rise. You will fall."

"How is it that Pax will prove he is worthy?"

"He must stand before the Majlis Alkahana and be judged. Let's begin!"

Ukweli turned and ran toward Pax only to be seized and bound by Yazata. The large demon from the basement, whose name was Rasul, also appeared and began to pronounce sayings toward Ukweli that kept him bound and silent.

As Pax stood in the middle of the garden, twelve large bronze statues rose up from the earth, three on each side. Each statue had a face engraved in the bronze that chanted praises to the sun god.

From the island of Atum, from the waters of Nun, all praises to Ra!

Pax intended to run but stood still instead. He didn't understand everything that was happening, but he knew his father needed him. He had never seen anything like this, but his coin flips had taught him there was more to life than what he could experience with his senses. He decided to be brave. Besides, he couldn't see an alternative.

The goddess stood beside Pax and spoke.

"These are the twelve honorable members of Majlis Alkahana. They will each pose one challenge to test the worthiness of Virtus Pax Aseyori as a proper conduit for Ma'at and a proper seed for Ra. To receive favor from the god of creation, Virtus Pax must successfully complete all twelve challenges to the satisfaction of the honorable members of the Majlis Alkahana." The goddess forcefully grabbed Pax by the arm and reached into his jacket pocket for the coin. "I'll take this. We wouldn't want you cheating, now, would we." She sat the coin on a half column just off the grass to the west of the garden. "Let's begin."

Elder #1: *"Four men are wearing hats . . ."*

Pax: "The second man speaks."

Elder #1: *"Defend."*

Pax: "The two men facing the wall are irrelevant. When the third man doesn't speak, the second man knows his hat is different from the first man, so he speaks."

Elder #2: *"What is pi?"*

Pax: "The question is ambiguous. Given the context of the trial, I'm assuming you're not referring to the baked dish, and while I'm tempted to say pi is equal to 3.141592653 and so on, I would guess you would say that is the *value* of pi. So, I'll say that pi is the ratio of the circumference of a circle to its diameter."

Elder #3: *"When a variable star pulsates radially . . ."*

Pax: "Cepheid."

Elder #4: *"What are the four quantum numbers?"*

Pax: "Principal. Azimuthal. Magnetic. Spin."

Elder #5: *"What name is given to an enzyme that fragments DNA at specific sites within molecules?"*

Pax: "Restriction endonuclease."

Elder #6: *"Qui victor fuit in pugna lacus Regillus?"*

Pax: "Victor dux apud Regillum lacum A. Postumius Albus pugnatum est."

The goddess rolled her eyes.

Elder #7: *"From whom did the Indian Mahatma Gandhi and the American Martin Luther King Jr. derive their ideas concerning civil disobedience?"*

Pax: "Henry David Thoreau."

Pax suddenly found himself falling until he landed with a splash into dark, turbulent water. The wind was strong and the waves tossed him violently about. He secured his bearing and began to tread water. He could taste salt in the water, and he could see an abundance of stars. There was darkness all around, but the moonlight was bright and shimmered off the water thanks to a clear sky.

Elder #8: *"There is a small island six hundred meters in the direction of the moonlight. You have twelve minutes before the predators among you are licensed to feast. Swim, or die."*

Pax began to swim in the direction of the moonlight and found that the waves and the wind were working against him. Knowing that a surface swim under these conditions would be impossible, he swam just beneath the surface and only came up periodically for air and to get his bearings. As he felt his body beginning to fatigue, he imagined the creatures that were pursuing him, eagerly awaiting the dinner bell. He swam as hard as he could, just under the surface of the water. He had no idea how long he had been swimming when he noticed a large shark in the water beside him. Pax was relieved to feel sand under his feet just before the voice of the elder instructed the predators to feast. He ran ashore, barely escaping the clutching jaws of the beast at his ankle, and hugged the single palm tree. He was immediately returned to the garden, still wet from the swim.

Elder #9: *"Is this a dagger which I see before me, the handle toward my hand?"*

Pax: "Come, let me clutch thee. I have thee not, and yet I see thee still."

Elder #10: *"What term describes the force that acts on an object for a finite period of time causing a change in the object's momentum?"*

Pax: "A change in momentum is caused by an impulse."

Pax was suddenly standing in front of a man dressed in black. The man's face was covered except for his eyes, and he stood in a fighting pose.

Elder #11: *"Fight or die!"*

The man in black charged at Pax and threw a series of punches, which he was able to dodge. Pax ducked under a kick before jumping over a leg sweep. As Pax backed away, the man continued to approach and threw more punches. which Pax blocked. He countered with punches of his own, but the man dodged and blocked them all. He gained leverage over Pax and grabbed him from behind, but Pax struck the man with the back of his head twice and kicked him in the abdomen with the back of his heel until he released him. Pax fell to the ground and rolled to a stand. The man attacked, and Pax dropped to a split and punched the inside of his right knee, causing him to tumble. After regaining his balance, the man attacked again and Pax slipped the punches before countering with strikes to the man's groin and chest. While the man was bent over, Pax delivered a flying knee to his face and he fell to the ground. Pax quickly positioned himself behind the man and secured a wrist lock chokehold until he fell unconscious. Pax stood and the man vanished from the garden.

Elder #12: *"What is the most noble of human experiences?"*
Pax: "Sacrifice."
Elder #12: *"The show of mercy."*

The god and goddess walked to the middle of the garden and stood in front of Pax. The god began to laugh as the goddess spoke.

"Oh, so close! You're a very impressive young man. Who knew you would survive eleven elders? I can see your father's influence on you, though. Only a fool would think sacrifice is a superior ethic! It's clear that sacrifice *ends* the human experience. The most noble of human experiences is the acquisition of great power and the consequent show of mercy to your conquered foes. For it is written, I desire mercy, and not sacrifice. Not that it matters now. Your life is mine to claim, and soon, so will your father's!"

Ukweli, still bound, began to shake his head. He felt the power growing inside of him. He didn't know what was happening to him, but he knew he wasn't about to let them take his son. The more belligerent he grew, the more the power revealed itself until finally a dark fluid began to cover his body. It emerged from his hands and completely obscured his form. He let out a scream and all twelve members of the Majlis Alkahana shook violently before crumbling to the ground.

The god Ra stood with his eyes wide open and began to celebrate. "It is time! The dark power has overtaken him! Now, my queen. Become one with him, and know the power of the darkness at the center of the sun!"

The goddess walked calmly, regally, and stood before Ukweli. "Don't worry, this won't hurt a bit." She kissed him and began to absorb the darkness. As Ra celebrated, the priests were slowly resurrected and began to chant, *Praise be to the goddess who lives forever! Power and Order!*

In the midst of the chaos, no one noticed Pax ease over to the half column where the goddess had placed his coin. As he reached for it, the god Ra screamed and lunged quickly toward him. Just before the god could place his hands on Pax, he flipped the coin. The landscaped distorted and the god froze in space. Everything went dark.

When Pax opened his eyes, he was sitting beside his father on the shore of the Nile, watching the boats sail by. "You know, I used to go to the canal in Islington and watch the boats. That's where I met your mom."

"Dad, we have to go!"

Ukweli was bewildered. "Wait, what do you mean?"

Pax's urgency grew. "Dad, now!"

Pax started running toward the truck. Ukweli got up and ran after him. Just as they got in, Ukweli could see the bold shape and colors of Yazata coming over the horizon.

"What is happening?" Ukweli found himself looking to his son for guidance.

Pax spoke with energetic clarity. "Dad, it's a trap. They were never going to empower you. They're trying to steal your abilities for themselves!"

Ukweli, still struggling to understand, lightly touched Pax on the shoulder. "Who's trying to steal my abilities? What abilities?"

"Ma'at and Ra!" Pax realized he was shouting.

"Wait, how do you know this? Is that why Yazata is after us?"

Pax took a deep breath to calm his heart rate. "I'll fill in the blanks later. Just please hurry!"

Ukweli pressed the gas and made a quick escape

through the city to the tarmac at Kibrit. Once he and Pax were safely in the air, Ukweli had questions.

"Okay, Pax, what the hell is going on?"

Pax scrunched his face and put his hand under his chin. "I'm not sure where to start."

"Start at the beginning."

The flight attendant stepped out of the cabin. "Captain, what can I get for you?"

Ukweli, still adamantly seeking answers, was gracious. "Nothing right now, Lacy. Thank you." She went back through the cabin door.

Pax began his recollection. "Well, do you remember that coin Mrs. Bergstrom gave me?"

"Vaguely. What does that have to do with anything?" Ukweli was growing weary of what seemed to be a series of meaningless facts.

Pax continued. "Well, one day you and Mom were arguing right outside my bedroom door, so I put on my headphones and listened to a song called 'Flip a Coin.' It's one of PonyTail's songs."

"Ugh, whatever. Okay, and then?" Ukweli resisted the urge to roll his eyes.

Pax continued. "Then, I flipped the coin. The room started spinning. When it stopped, you and Mom were still arguing."

"So?"

"But it was the same part of the argument you just had."

"Are you saying . . ."

"Yes, when I flip the coin, I go back in time."

"That's ridiculous." Ukweli shook his head in disbelief.

"I thought so, too, but it's true."

"Prove it."

"There's no way for me to prove it to you. Ra and Ma'at could sense it. But you never have."

"You've done this before?"

"A few times."

"How far back in time do you go?"

"It has generally been six seconds, but tonight was different. Perhaps the emotion of the moment extended the dilation."

"So, Ra and Ma'at knew you had the ability to reverse time with a coin and they just let you do it?"

"Ma'at took the coin from me before the trials began, but I got it back when she was busy draining your dark power."

"Trials? Dark power?" Ukweli tightened his countenance and sat up in his seat.

"Yes! They made you believe you were working with the World Society, when all this time they were just using you for your dark power. You are the son of Ra, and they want your power."

"So where do you come into all this?"

"I'm not sure if they can use my abilities, so it seems they just want to destroy me. You stopped them, though."

"I stopped them? How?"

"You used dark power. It's formidable, because it destroyed the priests who were conducting my trials. But it seems your dark power conflicts with the light in you. They've been waiting for the darkness to overtake the light. It happened when you saw me in danger."

"So, my dark power emerged to save you, and Ra was trying to take it?"

"Ma'at was taking it. Ra just seemed extraordinarily pleased."

"Then you flipped your coin."

"Yes, and we ended up back on the shore of the Nile."

"We're gonna need help, but there's no way to know who we can trust. We have a bastion in Nicosia. We can land there and make plans. I'll go ahead and start assembling the team now. This is short notice, even for Seers."

"Oh, and I know you're going to order fish and vegetables."

"Huh?"

"You're going to ask Lacy for fish and vegetables."

"How could you possibly know that?"

"This isn't the first time we've had this conversation." Pax wore a smirk that almost prompted Ukweli to threaten him with a spanking.

"Okay, I'm not crazy about that. Don't make it a habit."

"It doesn't matter. You'll never know I did it unless I tell you." Pax settled in with haughty satisfaction.

Ukweli pressed the small button on the side of his seat and a few moments later Lacy emerged.

"Fish and vegetables for me, please. Chicken for the kid. Thank you."

"Very good, sir. I'll have that momentarily." Lacy nodded and walked back behind the curtain.

As the plane flew over the Mediterranean toward Cyprus, Ukweli had a moment to ponder the new revelations. The more he thought, the more questions he had.

"Tell me again about the priests who were conducting your trials?"

"They came out of the ground. They were like statues, but they had faces and expressions and they praised Ma'at and Ra." Pax used his hands to manipulate his expressions.

"What kind of trials did they conduct as statues?"

"They mainly asked questions. They said they were testing my worthiness."

"Worthiness for what?"

"Worthy to be the seed for the family line. I think it was all a ruse to get you to genuinely believe I was in mortal danger."

Ukweli nodded. "In order to draw out the dark power?"

"Yes. Now I have a question—how are you familiar with that thing that was chasing us?"

"That was a demon. He calls himself Yazata. He serves the goddess Mithras. I have encountered him before. He's very formidable, and he's not the only one."

Pax angled his head and looked up. "Is it possible Mithras and Ma'at are the same goddess?"

Ukweli shrugged. "I'm not sure, but that was definitely Yazata, so I guess it's possible."

Lacy came from around the corner with a large carrier and stopped it in front of Ukweli. She locked the wheels and began to remove the contents.

"Fish for the gentleman." She placed Ukweli's plate on the table in front of him. "And chicken for the cutie." Pax smiled. Lacy placed the plate on the table in front of Pax. "Is there anything else I can help either of you with?"

Ukweli smiled. "I think we're okay, Lacy. Thank you."

When Lacy disappeared behind the short wall, Ukweli and Pax began to eat.

"When you ordered chicken for me, I assumed it would be fried," Pax spoke with chicken in his mouth.

"Yeah, you're very . . . mature for your age. Grilled chicken is better for you."

"Fried chicken tastes better to me."

"Fried chicken tastes better to everyone. Please chew and swallow before you talk." Ukweli and Pax were startled to hear a voice from behind them. They both turned. Ukweli immediately recognized the face. Pax didn't. "Unity."

"Hello, Ukweli. Hi, Pax. You sure are growing up to be a handsome young man."

"I don't think we've met." Pax spoke slowly and softly.

Unity sat beside Pax. "We haven't. I'm Unity. I'm a friend of your dad's."

Ukweli recognized that Unity's presence meant danger. Normally, he would just prepare for battle, but this was different. Pax was here. "Unity, if you're here, then we have—"

Unity interrupted. "Incoming. We're about to fly into a storm." Unity was always straight to business.

Ukweli was confused. "The pilots said our flight was clear into Nicosia."

Unity turned to face Ukweli directly and spoke emphatically. "It was. Now it's not. It seems there was supernatural intervention." Unity made her way toward the cockpit.

Ukweli sighed. "How much time do we have?"

Unity stopped with her hand on the cockpit door handle. "Thirty seconds. I'll go help the pilots divert. We'll have to get away from the water."

Ukweli removed his napkin. "And land where?"

Unity thought for a moment. "We'll have to turn east. It's the quickest way off the water. We can land in Tel Aviv."

"What should I expect when we hit the ground?" Ukweli had grown accustomed to Unity's presence in tense moments and, with Pax on board, feared her response.

Unity was somber. "The fight of your life. Literally."

(16)

TEL AVIV

The storm was intense and sudden. It wasn't hard to believe there was supernatural power behind it. The plane shook and the turbulence was more erratic than anything Ukweli had felt before. The drops were dramatic and unsettling, and he thought the plane might fall right out of the sky at any moment. He was tempted to enter the cabin and fly the plane himself—he certainly didn't trust the pilots to get them through this—but if anyone could, better than him, it was Unity.

Ukweli just sat as calmly as he could. He wanted to be strong for Pax. He was certain his son would be overtaken by fear, and he wanted to model what it meant to be strong. He was surprised to notice Pax sitting calmly beside him, watching a physics lecture. Ukweli always knew there was something special about him. He was learning there was much more to Pax than he had ever realized.

Eventually, the plane stabilized and Ukweli knew they were leaving the air over the sea. They landed safely at Ben Gurion, and it was Unity's plan to move toward Jerusalem.

"Why Jerusalem?" Ukweli asked.

"We need to get away from the water. The gods get power from the sea, as in the last days."

"That raises more questions."

"We will need help in this battle. We will find it there."

As the group traveled the hour from the airport to Jerusalem, Unity had somber warnings for Ukweli.

"You should prepare your heart and mind for the battle ahead."

"I've been in battles all my life, Unity." Ukweli tried not to sound arrogant.

"Not like this. Things are not as they seem, Captain." Unity shook her head.

"Oh, yeah? How so?"

"Please believe me. You will be faced with strong difficulties in this battle. Your enemies are many. Your enemies are close." Unity's concern was clear.

"I don't understand."

"You will. Prepare your heart. This will be an emotional fight. We will need high ground." As the vehicle raced through the outskirts of Jerusalem, the sky suddenly became black and the van was forced off the road by a mighty wind and into a sprawling garden, where they eventually crashed into a large Jerusalem pine. "It is time, Captain. Find your strength. Elevate your vision."

Ukweli turned around to get a visual of Pax, who was in the process of unbuckling his seatbelt.

"Pax, stay here. I'll come back for you when it's safe."

"Dad, let me come. I can help." Pax continued to unbuckle.

"No, it's far too dangerous. Please, just stay hidden. And stay quiet." Pax reluctantly relented.

As Unity and Ukweli stepped out of the vehicle, they looked around at the lush greenery and realized they were in an olive orchard. They navigated the vines to a clearing and found themselves face-to-face with Yazata and Rasul. The two massive figures pulsated shimmering, multicolored light as they waited to be released like pit bulls tugging at a chain. Ukweli could feel the energy inside him practically begging to get out. He prayed to encourage himself and to calm the dark energy. "But you, O Lord, are a shield about me, my glory, and the lifter of my head."

As he prayed, the demons began to laugh. Yazata said, "He who embraces the spoils of darkness now supposes to bow to light!"

Rasul responded, "If then the light in you is darkness, how great is the darkness!"

Suddenly, from the dark sky, Amon Ra descended cloaked in a dark cloud. When the cloud dissipated, the sun god stood with the goddess by his side. Ra maneuvered to the background with his hands raised as the goddess approached Ukweli in the clearing.

"Captain, you need only surrender the dark power and all you love will be saved." As she spoke, an army of torqs fell from the sky like so many droplets of rain during a summer storm. In an instant, ten thousand torqueo anima stood behind the goddess, prepared for battle. "As you can see, there is no other alternative."

Ukweli could feel the darkness rising as the fear paved a path for arrogance. "You have only increased the greatness of my triumph."

The goddess rolled her eyes. "Okay, let's end the games." She snapped her fingers and two large black vans drove into the grove and pulled to a stop. "Let's see if your hubris remains."

The doors of the first vehicle opened and Mendoza got out, followed by Kip and Kiera, who was holding Gabby. Two large torqs entered the clearing escorting Pax with his hands bound behind him. One torq held Pax while the other carried the coin and placed it in the hands of the goddess. Mendoza forced Kiera to the ground, along with the children, and held a gun to her back. Mendoza said, "Ukweli, just cooperate. You can see that you are beaten. You can't win, and the only way of escape is through the mercy of the goddess."

Ukweli was dismayed. "Claire, I . . . I trusted you."

"Ukweli, my loyalty lies with the goddess. She showed me the way of truth when I was just a child. Everything I have done in my life was to please her. Everything I have is because of her. And now, I am so close to having all that she has promised. So please, just give her what is due her and you can save your family." She slowly dropped her head and closed her eyes. "You can save us all." She paused before whispering, "Please."

Ukweli turned to see the doors of the second vehicle open. He was surprised to see Dakota and Bryce exit, followed by Millie and Penny. The women stood behind the children and suddenly forced them to their knees at gunpoint. Ukweli was disturbed and confused.

"Millie! Penny! What . . . what is this?"

Penny smiled as Millie spoke. "We are loyal servants of Mithras, and we have come so that she may claim what is rightfully hers!"

"But Millie, Penny . . . your children? Would you sacrifice the lives of your very own children?"

The goddess giggled as she addressed Ukweli. "Of course, they would never harm their own children. Fortunately, for them, these aren't their children." As the goddess moved, there was a smoky, silver shadow that followed her form. She walked over to Bryce and lifted his chin. "This handsome lad hails from the land of Djibouti. He became orphaned when the tactical team from the Church of the Seer, led by you, Captain Aseyori, stormed his compound and killed his family. You know, Kelley Jack, as cold and brash as she was, simply couldn't bring herself to follow the simplest of instructions. So, rather than terminate the child, she tossed him in the garbage, thinking she would give him the same chance she had as an infant. And now, here he is, once again a pawn in your game."

"A pawn in *my* game? Have I summoned us all here?"

"Ukweli, you're so dramatic. Yet the plot thickens." The goddess released Bryce and floated over to Dakota. She pulled a dagger from her side hilt and placed it at his throat. "And this young lad is my favorite person in this whole outrageous story. Dakota was presented to Millie and Parker as a personal gift from the DayStar. Jackson took the child straight from the womb of its mother and made her believe the child to be stillborn. Actually, get this, Dakota Williams was born July 20, 2043—the lovechild of Captain Ukweli Aseyori and the very married Kiera Connaught. That's right, Kiera. This is your son." Kiera, shocked, began to cry. "Oh, boohoo. I feel like Maury Povich! Ukweli, you *are* the father!"

Ukweli thought back and couldn't make himself believe he could have a child in Atlanta and not be aware. As he looked around, his family at gunpoint, his children in danger, and an army of ten thousand torqs facing him, he hung his head. He no longer had the strength to resist the fear, the anger, or the power of the growing darkness. His heart raced and he once again felt the searing fire flowing through his veins. He closed his eyes and knelt to the ground. When he opened them, they were black like onyx and his vision was supernatural. He could suddenly see past the bright colors of Yazata and the dark shroud around

Rasul, and his eyes fixed on the legion of demons at the center of the figures. He spoke Arabic, the language of his father.

"Yusharifuni 'ana 'unhiaka." (*I am honored to end you.*)

The demons trembled, but ran toward Ukweli to attack him, only to be caught in a chokehold. Ukweli held his hands in the air and squeezed his fists as the demons, still twenty feet from him, began to struggle for breath. He held each demon and squeezed until they went limp. There was a loud bang as Ukweli clapped his hands together. The demons dissolved into a mist and floated into the dark sky with a loud shriek. Ukweli now carried the appearance of a shadow as his transition to the darkness reached maturity. The goddess approached him and began to kiss him. Ukweli grew weak and could sense the dark power being drained from him, but he was powerless to stop it. They had done it. Yazata and Rasul had served their ultimate purpose. They had enticed the darkness to emerge in a moment of weakness and doubt, and it was exactly what they had planned. The previous attempts by the gods to reveal and subsequently absorb Ukweli's dark power had proven to be ineffective. The darkness lacked maturity. They had allowed the power to fully develop, even at the cost of valuable resources. They had come with a plan. They had executed the plan. And now, as he fell to the ground, Ukweli realized he could do nothing to stop what was coming. In fact, he tried to move and found himself unable. They had his family. They had his power. They could take over the world and there was no one to stand in their way.

As Ukweli allowed himself to sink into a depression of immobility, he heard the movement of air behind him. It was the circulation of the rotors of a helicopter as the large Chinook landed behind him. He couldn't move, but his spirits were lifted when Unity, now kneeling beside him, whispered into his ear, "Your help is here."

The large door at the rear of the transport opened and the members of Church of the Seer Elite emerged. Adam, Paul, Kei, and Charlotte stood in full armor ready for battle. Behind them, exiting the chopper last, was Mrs. Bergstrom carrying weapons in both hands.

The goddess, now possessing the great power she had sought for so long, a power promised to her by the sun god, was moderately amused at the show of force. She stepped to the side and, with a slight gesture, ordered the forward charge of her company of torqueo anima.

The torqs charged forward into the direct fire from the Elite Seers. Kei led the way with Adam and Paul following closely behind. They slashed and fired into the crowd with ferocity and precision. Charlotte stood behind the attack and controlled two missile-equipped drones that rained fire down on the demon-driven machines. The Elite Seers created a symphony of explosions and gunfire accompanied by the shriek of dissolving demons that was beautiful music in Ukweli's ears. He was proud of his team. He was thankful for them.

As the Seers fought their way through the hoard of torqs, Ukweli struggled to regain the strength to move. He managed to hold his head up long enough to see the goddess approach Kiera. The goddess lifted her from her crouched position and stood her upright. After looking her up and down, she reasoned aloud.

"The light that opposes the darkness. You have failed. All along, the darkness in Ukweli was drawn to its true nature. The siren tapped into Ukweli's essence, and he became more powerful than he ever could have been with you." The goddess lifted her hand and, with the movement of her fingers, drew Mendoza to her side. "It was the allegiance and persistence of the siren that made this all possible. It was she who enabled my access to your home and into your lives. She has done a great work and has duly earned compensation. Let me show her how much I appreciate her sacrifice."

The goddess opened her mouth and her eyes turned frosty black. She began to drain the lifeforce from Mendoza as she screamed in agony. Ukweli could only watch in terror as the aubergine energy flashed and flowed away from Mendoza until she finally fell to the ground. Mendoza was able to turn her head and look toward Ukweli in time to silently mouth, *I'm sorry.* As a single tear escaped the corner of her eye, she took her last breath.

Ukweli's eyesight began to fail and he laid his head flat on the ground just before losing consciousness. As he blacked out, he began to dream of Lagos and his family, and he saw visions of his childhood home. As he maneuvered around the familiar setting, he noticed a bright light coming from his old bedroom. He approached the door, turned the knob, and slowly pushed it open. He was surprised to see Ava.

"UK."

Ukweli cautiously approached Ava and reached out to touch her. "Is this . . . is this real? Am I in Caelum?"

Ava stepped toward him, gave him a hug, and held his hands. She smiled. "You're so handsome. I have missed you."

Ukweli fell to his knees with his face toward the ground. "I'm not worthy, Ava. I have failed."

Ava reached to lift him up. "Success makes you worthy?"

"All I hold dear is in peril. I failed you, and now Kiera, my children, my friends—they are all in danger because of me. I wasn't strong enough for you, or for them."

She lightly placed her left hand on the side of Ukweli's face and her right hand on his chest. "This isn't about strength, UK. It's about fear. You have too much fear."

Ukweli lifted his face to challenge Ava's assertion. "You know me better than that. I fear no man."

"You fear the suffering of those you love. Fear nourishes darkness."

"My power was in the darkness. There's no way I can defeat the goddess now."

"You are far more powerful than you realize."

"But I can't even move. My strength has faded."

"Did Nehemiah write, 'The darkness is your strength'?"

Ukweli smiled at the thought of Ava using sarcasm. "No, Ava."

"Then release your fear and pursue the joy of the Lord. All is well. The light remains. Quit bitching and square up!" Ava quickly punched Ukweli's face, and he suddenly found himself in the orchard in Jerusalem. As he regained consciousness, he found that his strength was growing.

Kiera, still in the grasp of the goddess, was losing hope. She felt the restraints of the goddess and she knew it was too much for her to escape. There was no reason to fight anymore. Ukweli had been rendered powerless. Pax and Kip were in bondage. The Seers were fighting against what seemed to be an insurmountable flow of torqs. She had no doubt they would soon be overrun and defeated by the tsunami of enemies. Then there was Millie, holding a firearm to the head of the child she never knew she had. And at the end of it all, she could see Gabby, lying calmly on the ground next to the corpse of her recently deceased mother.

The scene was overwhelming, so Kiera closed her eyes and began to pray. "Thysia, I have failed. I have not been to Ukweli what you have called me to be. The darkness has prevailed."

The goddess heard the prayer of surrender that Kiera uttered in that moment and began to celebrate. "You have done well to recognize the rise of the goddess. Everlasting power is mine!"

She went silent as Kiera uttered the closing words of her prayer. "Yet you, Thysia, remain."

The goddess was angered and drew Kiera close. She looked into Kiera's soul only to find that the light was indeed . . . growing. The goddess squeezed both hands together, attempting to drain the life from Kiera, but the more she squeezed, the more the light grew. She released her hold on Kiera and allowed her to fall to the ground.

Fear began to show in her countenance. "Impossible. You don't possess the authority to resist."

It was then that a bright light from the sky emerged through the darkness and the goddess recognized the voice of the archangel Michael. "Sto onoma tis thysias to fos pyerischyei!" (*In the name of the sacrifice, the light prevails!*) Kiera was only able to perceive the angel as a mass of light that descended to the earth and stood beside Ukweli just as he found the strength to stand. The angel looked toward Ukweli and yelled, "Epithesi!" (*Engage!*) The two of them moved quickly through the army of torqs completely and, seemingly, all in a single moment. The shrieks were heard in an instant and the entire remaining army of torqueo anima fell, motionless.

The god Ra and the goddess Mithras approached the archangel in the air to confront him.

The god spoke. "How is it that you have come to the defense of the man?"

The goddess spoke. "Has the man not carried the darkness

since his youth? Has he not embraced the darkness? Yet you respond with the destruction of my legions on his behalf?"

The archangel spoke. "Yea, the darkness hideth not from thee; But the night shineth as the day. The darkness and the light are both alike to thee."

The god spoke. "What then of justice?"

The goddess spoke. "Would you stand in the way of proper justice for the man?"

The archangel spoke. "Justice and judgment are the habitation of thy throne."

The god spoke. "This—"

Suddenly, the light summoned the god Ra and the goddess Mithras closer to him and they were compelled to bow in submission. The archangel spoke. "Sto onoma tis thysias epistrepste amesos!" (*In the name of the sacrifice, return immediately!*) The god and the goddess reluctantly clasped hands and walked into the light. The light disappeared into the sky with a flash.

Adam and Paul secured Millie and Penny and loaded them into the transport. Charlotte went to Kiera and found her exhausted but recovering. Mrs. Bergstrom tended to Pax and Kip, as she had always done. Kei went to Ukweli and found him collapsed and, again, barely able to move. With his family and his team now surrounding him, he prepared to enter his rest. He was sure that this was his final battle. He was able to move his head but felt himself losing strength as if it were seeping out of his pores. He felt the weight of so much violence in the name of the Church of the Seer. He always believed he was doing the right thing, or at least the noble thing. But now, he only felt ignorant for having been led by the spirit of darkness, which had been a part of him since birth. *Darkness was my destiny*, he thought. Barely able to speak, he said, "Fitting, with everything I've done, this seems the most appropriate end." Knowing his family was now safe from the goddess, he closed his eyes and made his peace. "I love you all. Until we meet again."

His sight began to fade and his breathing became labored. Kiera and Pax came to his side and embraced him with tears. But it was Kip who spoke. "Wait, Daddy." She lay beside him and wrapped herself in his arms as she had done so many times on the living room sofa in Zurich. As she lay, however, Ukweli's strength began to return. He could feel his lungs expanding as they took in air. His eyes started to focus and he was able to move his arms and legs. Eventually, he was able to sit up, and he embraced Kip for a few moments more before he was able to stand. In shock, he knelt in front of her.

"Kip, baby, what did you do for me?"

"You were hurting, so I made it better."

"You did, you did!" Ukweli picked Kip up over his head and swung her around before giving her a big hug and a kiss.

Everyone joined in the embrace as Ukweli, his friends, and his family all loved on each other. The embrace was interrupted by a blinding white light that radiated from the midst of the group. The light was so bright that it forced everyone to step back and look away. As the light began to dim, the imposing yet gentle figure of Thysia stood. It felt natural for everyone to bow down with their faces to the ground, and they all did. Everyone remained bowed except Ukweli, whose face was lifted by the touch of Thysia.

"I have prayed for you that your faith would not fail. And when you have turned again, strengthen your brothers."

As all the others lay prostrate with their faces to the ground, Ukweli kneeled in the presence of Thysia. He said, "Not my will, my Lord." He bowed with humility.

"This world will need your faith. You will be rejected. Nevertheless, keep Hope, for I have overcome the world."

At that time Hope appeared beside Ukweli and embraced him softly. Noticing that Hope was present, he wept with staggered breath. "Please, Hope, what is it? What has my sin cost?"

Hope hugged him again. "Your sin is covered."

"Yet you have come to console me." Ukweli gently pushed away from her. She smiled at him before stepping away and kneeling in front of Kiera.

Thysia placed his left hand on Ukweli's shoulder. "Suffer little children, and forbid them not, to come unto me: for of such is the kingdom of heaven." It was only then that Ukweli noticed Thysia was holding Gabby in his right arm.

Ukweli dropped his chin to his chest. "You're taking Gabrielle from me."

Hope returned to Ukweli and lifted his face. "You're returning Gabrielle to Him. She was always *His*."

Ukweli felt angry and his first instinct was to fight, but the presence of Thysia emitted a suffocating love that carried an aroma that infiltrated his senses and compelled obedience in the face of uncertainty. Still, Ukweli attempted to bargain. "Please, my Lord, take me instead."

"Your work continues. This little one will enter the Father's presence."

Ukweli experienced the greatest comfort he had ever known, yet, out of his humanity, he expressed anguish. "Please be gracious to me. I cannot endure."

Thysia smiled and touched Ukweli on the side of his face. "Don't let your heart be troubled. Believe in God, believe also in me." Ukweli suddenly remembered the conversation he had with Mendoza in Atlanta about trusting others with Gabby's care. It dawned on him that if he would trust Gabby in Kiera's hands, he should certainly trust Gabby to be loved and safe in the arms of Thysia.

With Gabby's tiny hands playing with his beard, Thysia turned and walked into a distorted cloudy effect. Ukweli stared and cried silently. As the tears poured down, he was barely able to observe as Thysia kissed Gabby on the cheek before handing her to Mara. Ukweli saw his mother welcome Gabby to Caelum. Mara embraced Gabby, then turned and gently passed her to Uzuri. There was, suddenly, a great flash of light that caused Ukweli to turn away. When he turned back, the effect was gone. Thysia was gone. Hope was gone. Gabby was gone. Ukweli wiped the tears from his face as he spoke softly to himself, "I will go to her, but she will not return to me."

17

ACCOUNTABILITY

DECEMBER 17, 2052

U kweli sat in front of a large wooden table facing Georgia Superior Court Justice Fredrick Wilhite. Ukweli had been apprehended upon reentering the United States from Israel and he was about to be questioned by attorneys for the World Society. He sat and listened to Tommie Walker testify that he was a witness to Ukweli killing Brad Hassan in cold blood in his home in what he described as a "passionate rage." The president of Mongolia said Ukweli and his then wife, Ava Sanusi, had taken advantage of the country's hospitality while murdering several of its citizens, including the prime minister, the PM's chief of staff Claire Mendoza, by whom Ukweli had illegitimately fathered a now deceased daughter, and several peaceful desert dwellers. A spokesman for the royal estate of Djibouti said that video evidence showed that Ukweli and his loyal hoard of renegades had unlawfully entered their compound and murdered the entire family, including men, women, children, staff, and animals, with malice. Millie Williams and Penny James testified that the Aseyori household was dysfunctional and abusive, and that Pax was some manner of mad scientist and possibly a terrorist. The mayor of Atlanta testified that Ukweli's trail of bodies would reach from Stonecrest to Villa Rica. President James said he was appalled at Ukweli's audacity. He testified that he had mistakenly trusted Ukweli and was distraught that an American citizen would embarrass him in front of the entire planet by betraying the trust of the World Society. Charles Connaught explained that Ukweli had impregnated his daughter-in-law twice and killed his son. He testified that his son, Jackson, was somewhat of a childhood rival of Ukweli's, but that "Mr. Aseyori" had never let it go. "I think Mr. Aseyori allowed his jealousy of my son's political success to fester until he was motivated to commit murder in front of a live television audience," he said.

As Ukweli prepared to take the stand, Judge Wilhite suddenly asked him to remain in his seat. He then proceeded to inform the court, "In light of the overwhelming abundance of evidence against Captain Aseyori, I find him guilty of crimes against humanity and do therefore sentence him to home arrest for a minimum of two years and not to exceed five, under the jurisdiction of the World Society."

The High Council seized control of the Church of the Seer headquarters building in Atlanta, though Charlotte had already moved the weapons and resources. The Society assumed control of the aircraft and placed severe restrictions on the type of contact Ukweli could have with his team members. His movements and communications were monitored almost nonstop.

DECEMBER 25, 2052

Ukweli and Kiera hosted a December Yuletide gathering at their home in Zurich. Mrs. Bergstrom prepared a traditional American holiday spread with turkey, ham, potatoes, green beans, baked macaroni and cheese, yams, pies, and unicorn-shaped chicken fingers with fries for Kip. The entire Elite squad was present, still sore and bruised from the epic battle just one week prior, but happy to gather under less stressful circumstances. Adam kept the event light with funny stories about Ukweli growing up in Islington. Paul jumped in with dark stories about combatting torqs. He thought they were funny, but no one laughed. Mrs. Bergstrom kept the champagne and hot chocolate flowing and Charlotte kept upbeat Yuletide-themed music on the sound system. There were gifts for the children. Kip really racked up. Ukweli had no idea that there was in existence such a volume of toys adorned with unicorns. Pax had only asked for training equipment, but Kei had been able to acquire a one-of-a-kind set of writings by Japanese theoretical physicist Hideki Yukawa on his prediction of the pi meson. Pax was so excited that he gave Kei a hug with a big smile.

There was, however, a sense of anxiety in the air. Dakota Williams, having been proven to be Ukweli and Kiera's son, had moved into the Aseyori household just the day before. They had gifts for him to open and he tried to seem happy, but he missed Millie and Parker. They had been the only family he had ever known. Ukweli had demanded, however, that Millie and Parker be given no access to Dakota. He just couldn't get past seeing Millie with a gun pointed at Dakota's back. Since Dakota was his son, Ukweli planned to raise him far away from the influence of Mithras and the World Society.

Bryce James was given the opportunity to be adopted away from Penny. Mrs. Bergstrom would've happily taken him in, and there were other families in town who volunteered. Surprisingly, Bryce chose to stay with Penny. It wasn't only because he was so familiar with her. It wasn't just because she was the only family he ever had. Bryce had heard the goddess say that Ukweli and the Seers had killed his family. The more he thought about it, the more he became intrigued with the teachings of Mithras and the power of Ra. He wanted to know more about the World Society and vowed to himself that one day he would access the power to avenge his family. Penny and Bryce planned a move to Egypt, where Bryce could learn Arabic and begin training to serve the goddess, closely monitored by the watchful eye of the World Society.

Though this would've only been Gabby's second December Yuletide celebration, her absence in the room was palpable. But no one felt the loss like Kiera. In the week since Gabby had been taken to Caelum, Kiera was distant. Ukweli had tried to describe what he had seen in his vision of Thysia giving Gabby to his mother, but Kiera hadn't seen it for herself and struggled to believe. Her faith had been tested and found wanting. She had failed. Her grief was deep-seated, and she tried to put on a strong face for Pax and Kip, but her performance was too pitiful to convince even herself. She held her champagne glass and she toasted when instructed. She clapped when Kip opened her presents. She watched Dakota move around and tried to make it make sense. *You lost Gabby, who wasn't yours, but you gained Dakota, who is yours.* She wanted to welcome him, but the more she tried, the more she realized she just didn't have the strength for it at the moment. It wasn't until she opened her present from the sprouts, a tree ornament with a picture of Gabby on it, that she truly allowed herself to feel the hurt. She smiled and hugged her children, and immediately dropped to her knees and began to cry.

Ukweli had not known what it was to be an instrument of emotional support for anyone. He didn't resist the urge, though, and when he saw his wife in distress, he didn't just jump to her rescue. He simply got on his knees beside her and allowed himself to join in her grief. So, Kiera and Ukweli cried together, in front of their friends and children, on their knees beside the ornamented tree during the December Yuletide gathering. For the first time in a long time, Ukweli felt free; he wasn't embracing Kiera out of masculine duty. And for the first time in a long time, Kiera felt loved and understood by her husband. For a few brief minutes, they were teenagers in the park in Islington. There was no mission. There was no darkness. There was grief, but there was comfort.

18

MOVING ON

Ukweli celebrated his thirty-third birthday by informing his team that he was officially retiring from the Church of the Seer. His demon-hunting days were over, and though he didn't trust the World Society, he figured they were someone else's problem now. With the darkness now expelled from his genetics, absorbed by the goddess, Ukweli had experienced a childlike innocence for the first time since the Company murdered his sister. He planned to spend the rest of his days doing what made him happy, which, for the most part, was making Kiera happy. He reorganized the soccer club in town and became the head coach, instructing both of his sons. Kiera became his assistant coach and Ukweli was surprised at her intensity. He knew her to be competitive, but found himself pulling her to the side from time to time just to calm her down and to provide breathing room for the referees. Kip joined the arts club downtown, the Dance Domain, and while Mrs. Bergstrom attended most of the rehearsals, Ukweli didn't miss a single recital. If he had to choose between a soccer game and a dance recital, he left the team in Kiera's capable hands while he put on his unicorn hat and headed to the dance. He loved being a girl dad, and he loved being Kiera's husband.

Of course, there were still questions concerning the supernatural abilities that his children possessed. Pax had learned from his research that he could move in time but was limited in his movement in space, meaning that regardless how far he traveled back in time, he would still occupy a similar space on the planet. If he flipped his coin in Zurich, he would travel back in time to a similar place. He also learned that he could travel forward in time, but never past a point he hadn't been. He could travel from fifteen minutes ago to eight minutes ago, but he couldn't travel to an as yet undetermined future. He struggled to understand the physics of it all. The dilations couldn't explain how his past becoming his present represented a new future. Ukweli wanted to understand Pax's abilities; he knew the old math, but the required new math hadn't been invented yet. Kip's abilities, however, were easier for him to understand. She was full of love and joy, and he wasn't surprised to learn that her love and joy had supernatural ramifications. Anyone who hugged Kip felt better, with or without superpowers.

Kiera loved Kip and Pax, and she was learning to love Dakota. It didn't take long for Ukweli to bond with Dakota, too. His sons were teammates and best friends. They reminded him of his relationship with his friends, and he found himself praying that they would be for each other what Adam and Paul had been to him. It would be another five years before Ukweli, and the World Society, would discover that Dakota also had a special ability.

JANUARY 20, 2053

The Fifth Presidential Inauguration of Barnabas Aloysius James took place in Washington, DC, with the heads of the World Society in attendance. There was all the pomp and grandeur expected at the coronation of a king, or perhaps a modern-day ceremony to install a dictator. The regional directors, called chancellors, sat on the stage behind the podium to represent the strength and solidarity of the World Society. As chairman of the High Council, Alexander Scott was given the honor of swearing in the president, and he gave a warm welcome to the world as he introduced President James. The president stepped to the bouquet of microphones and confidently looked into the hundreds of cameras directed at his position.

"Fellow citizens of these great United States of America, citizens of the North American territories, and yes, citizens of the glorious planet Earth, it is my honor to stand before you today to, once again, accept the heavy burden that is the mantle of leadership. I am eternally grateful that you have chosen me for an unprecedented fifth term in office. I am, as always, so proud of you for recognizing my leadership capabilities and trusting me as the one and only man who can lead us into our preferred future. This level of leadership is truly set apart for those who are chosen, not by you or me, but by the providence of the gods of the universe. The divine order has determined that I alone am worthy and capable of this office, and I, along with my colleagues at the World Society, will continue to lead this planet into the prosperity and peace destined long ago. Though our rule is absolute, our rule is yet benevolent. You are so fortunate to be so fortunate."

The crowd of nearly two million citizens gathered at the

National Mall began to cheer and chant back and forth, "Absolute benevolence!" For as often as societies descend into fascism, it is not by might and power or the agony of war, but by the approbation of the masses.

Ukweli and Kiera sat at the kitchen table with their luggage by the door. Ukweli had decided he wanted to celebrate his retirement by taking Kiera on a vacation. He understood he was being monitored by the World Society wherever in the world he happened to be, so he decided he would like to be monitored in Belize for a couple of weeks. Kiera wasn't thrilled about leaving her children behind, but she knew Mrs. Bergstrom would be on top of things. Besides, she needed this time with Ukweli. Everything about their adult relationship had been saturated with chaos and infidelity and dragons and demons, and she was ready, at long last, to put it all behind her. She had never stopped loving Ukweli, but she hoped they could return to an existence where she *liked* him. She could tell he was genuinely putting forth the effort to make her feel special, so she allowed herself to explore the possibilities of being in a fulfilling relationship. The thought excited her. Ukweli was grateful for an opportunity to make things right.

They addressed the sprouts to set expectations for behavior and responsibilities. They spoke with their kids on the danger of fire and the importance of minding Mrs. Bergstrom. They would be expected to continue in their chores and, of course, their training. The couple embraced their three children before heading to the car with their things. The children stood on the porch and watched their parents drive away. When they walked back into the house, they found Mrs. Bergstrom standing beside a man. Neither Kip nor Dakota recognized the man, but Pax knew who it was. Mrs. Bergstrom asked the children to take a seat before making a formal introduction.

"Children, now that your parents are off on their holiday, I would like to introduce you to a gentleman who will continue your learning and development. This is Alexander Scott."

The children were silent as Alexander pulled up a chair and sat in front of them.

"Listen, I know you don't know me, but—"

Pax interrupted, "I know you. You're the head of the World Society."

"Well, that's correct. Perhaps I have underestimated you."

"The World Society has been mean to my dad." Pax looked Alexander in the eye and Alexander took it as a show of respect.

Alexander explained. "Yes, well, that's why I'm here, young man. I was there in Rome with your parents in the days just before you were born. I remember the look on your father's face when he stepped off the plane in Atlanta holding you in his arms."

"Then why are you treating my dad unfairly?" Pax shrugged.

"Listen, Pax, there are things happening here that I know you can't possibly understand."

Mrs. Bergstrom said, "Ahem, I'm not so sure, Alexander. Pax passed the Trial of the Elders in Egypt. He is obviously more advanced than we thought."

"Maybe," Alexander never looked away from Pax, "but he can't understand it all."

"That's why you're here. Please, let's get started." Mrs.

Bergstrom handed Kip a pouch filled with peach yogurt and pulled her up on her lap. "You can address the boys. I'll take care of the young lady."

"Very well." Alexander asked the two boys to come closer. He lightly placed his hands on their foreheads and began to speak while the boys were given a vision of the stars. "Since the beginning of time, there has been a battle between the forces of good and evil. The creator God of the universe has always sought to influence mankind toward good things like love, joy, peace, patience, kindness, goodness, faithfulness, gentleness, and self-control. On the other hand, the opposition looks to influence men toward sexual immorality, impurity, idolatry, jealousy, and malice. As a boy, not much older than you two are right now, I was given a vision from the Spirit of God. It revealed to me that I must suffer greatly for the name of Thysia, but afterward I would be elevated to a place of power within the boundaries of the enemy. This enemy goes by many names, but they are all the same. You may know them as the Company, or possibly Imperium Intergalactic. Now, they are called the World Society, and they are influenced by the entity they call The Beautiful One. They seek the ultimate power, which gives them leverage over men's souls. Thysia has positioned me behind enemy lines to combat the forces of evil, but I can't do it alone."

The boys looked confused for a moment before Pax reentered the conversation. "That doesn't explain why you treat my dad like a criminal."

"The World Society considers powerful people and organizations as threats. They tried to get your father and the other Seers on board, but Thysia intervened. Your father's freedom makes him a target."

"Then why would you let them leave for holiday alone?"

"It is not your father's physical freedom they fear."

"Are my parents in danger?"

"Thysia has a hedge around your parents. The World Society, like the Company and Imperium before them, can only do what they are allowed to do."

Pax thought for a moment. "So why are you here with us?"

"I'm here because it is time for you to use your abilities in the service of Thysia. It is time for you to join the fight."

"How? What am I supposed to do?"

"I know you have done minimal development on your skill. You use your coin as a token to initiate and channel your time dilations."

"How do you know about that?"

"We have been monitoring you. The World Society is aware that you can manipulate time. They are not aware, however, of the depth of that particular ability. Honestly, neither are you."

"What do you mean?"

"What if I told you that you have the ability to change the fabric of the history of the world? To travel back to days, times, and places long past. To make a real difference."

"I would say you are mistaken. My dilations have only recently gone beyond six seconds. I assumed it was because of the stress of the moment."

"You assumed incorrectly. The greater the anxiety, the greater the chaos in your dilations. In order for you to travel through time and space, you will need to develop resolve. Uncontrolled emotions will lead to errors in placement."

"If I assume that to be true, I'm still very limited, as I am unable to experience dilations through locations. Time moves, but spaces don't."

"You are incorrect again—well, partially. While it is true that you alone can't experience dilations through space, you can travel through space with a navigator."

"I don't understand."

"As it turns out, your long-lost brother has a special ability as well. He is a navigator. While you have the ability to move through dilations in time, he has the ability to navigate spaces. The two of you, once you are developed, can travel through time *and* space."

Dakota politely raised his hand. "I don't understand any of this. Dilations, navigation . . . what does this all mean?"

Alexander placed his hand on Dakota's shoulder. "Have you ever imagined a place so vividly you felt like you were actually there? Have you tasted saltwater or smelled cedars only to realize you were daydreaming?"

"Of course, but I'm sure everyone does that."

"No, sir. As a navigator, your senses are attached to your visions. Where other people only perceive that they can smell the bread in their memory or dreams, you actually have the experience."

Pax spoke up. "So, I move in time and Dakota navigates the spaces."

"That is correct," Alexander confirmed.

Dakota was still confused and altogether unsure. "This sounds dangerous. What would we even do in a different time and space?"

Mrs. Bergstrom, still holding Kip in her lap, said, "It is very dangerous. That's where this precious darling comes into it."

Pax said, "What does any of this have to do with Kip? She's not even four years old."

Alexander responded, "She is young, but you can't do any of this without her."

"Why?" Pax was troubled to learn his destiny might require him to put his baby sister in harm's way.

Alexander turned to face Kip as he spoke. "This little one is the key to your survival. The time dilations at six seconds or fifteen seconds or two minutes have little effect on you and your physical body. However, dilations through time and space of multiple years, like the dilations you will be asked to frame, will technically tear your bodies right down to the atoms. There's no way for you to survive the dilations—at least, not without a regenerator. It is Kip and her abilities that will keep you from becoming scattered atoms when you dilate."

"So . . . Kip is a . . . healer?"

"Oh, she's much more than that. She can reorganize and rebuild the atoms within a cell. I hope I don't need to explain the ramifications."

"So, she can turn water into wine?"

"Better. She can separate the molecules and turn water into pure oxygen."

"So, she can breathe underwater?"

"If she needs to."

"Well, that's pretty cool." Pax was impressed.

"It is, until it isn't. Your missions will be very dangerous. And because your parents are always under surveillance, they can't know about your involvement."

Pax pondered this new information. He was willing to admit Alexander had provided answers to questions he hadn't been able to process for himself. But he still wasn't satisfied with Alexander's involvement in the first place. After all, if he really had his parents' best interests in mind, why would he align himself with the goddess? Why hadn't he stepped in before? Why was he just now entering the scene? "I don't really know how to feel."

Alexander stepped in to assure him. "Pax, think of it this way. Your father dedicated his life to fighting evil forces all over the globe because he wanted you and your sister to grow up in a world free from negative influences. He felt like a failure because it didn't matter how many torqs he slayed or how many governments he toppled; the influence of evil remained. He fought in the only way he knew how, with guns and swords. But you and Dakota and Kip, you will fight a smarter fight. By traveling in time to right wrongs, you will fight in the arena where the enemy's influence is most powerful—the hearts and minds of the citizens of the world. This is Thysia's destiny for you. And your training begins now."

EPILOGUE

The Beautiful One sat on a golden throne with a shiny golden scepter in his right hand. He wore a golden, diamond-encrusted crown on his head. There were ten steps from his throne down to the floor, where his audience was seated on either side of a rectangular stone table. On one side, the usual suspects—Jackson Connaught, Ann Jefferson, Jennifer Devore, and the demon Lapsus. On the other, Amon Ra, Mithras, Baal, and Dagon. The Beautiful One stood from his throne and made the walk down the stairs to the seat at the head of the stone table. Attendants removed his crown and cloak and took his scepter. He sat down and addressed the small gathering.

"I'm proud of you. I'm proud of your efforts. You have managed to subtly influence the planet of men to a single world currency under a single world administration. They are kings in their own eyes and take credit for things they don't even understand. The wealthy manipulate the downtrodden into believing they share their interests, and the poor respond by worshipping and further empowering the wealthy. They lie to themselves until the truth feels oppressive. They bow to whatever supports their personal delusions. Even those who claim to follow the Magician abandon his tenets for finances, popularity, or dopamine. Anything to maintain the status quo. So, yes, I'm proud of you.

"The Magician continues to unfairly alter the parameters of the contests in favor of the world of men, and they continue to respond by doing whatever feels right. So, let's keep chipping away. It doesn't matter how large the tree, eventually, one axe blow will send it tumbling to the ground. The Big Boss inexplicably gave the world of men dominion over the planet only for them to immediately hand it over to me. The Magician constantly oversteps his bounds, but it doesn't matter because the world of men continues to embrace the darkness. You all have made this possible.

"So now, as our enemies prepare to launch the weapon, let us lean on the tendency of men to choose contrary to their own well-being. Continue to present them with options. As always, the problem is choice. So long as we give them a dark option, they will abandon the Magician and make dark choices. It is simply their nature. Work to establish their nature as their norm. Convince them that if it feels natural, it must be right. That is how we will continue to prevail. The sacrifice of the Magician will only be a footnote in history."

"And you, sir, where will you be?"

"I'll be with you on the earth, going to-and-fro, walking up and down on it. But right now I have a meeting to attend. The Big Boss has summoned his sons, and I'm going to . . . check in."

ACKNOWLEDGMENTS

I thank God for each and every person who has ever supported the Church of the Seer series in any way. Though this story represents the close of the original trilogy and the end for so many characters we have come to know and love, I am excited about the future of the franchise. With new leaders boasting new and exciting abilities, the Church of the Seer is in capable hands!

I teach a Sunday School class on Facebook Live on Sundays at 10 a.m. EST, and I would be honored if you joined us!

If you have questions about the Church of the Seer books, the Bible, or if you have prayer requests, you can follow me on social media and contact me through direct messages. It would be my honor to engage with you! @kenyafouch

ABOUT THE AUTHOR

Kenya Fouch is a career educator and athletic administrator turned author. Kenya spent fifteen years in public education in a variety of areas, teaching math, history, economics, and physical education in addition to serving as a high school football coach for thirteen years and an athletic administrator for seven. Kenya started his own academic advising brand, 15, in 2019 and currently serves in the children's ministry and as a Sunday school teacher at his church.

Kenya is from Hartwell, Georgia, and attended Hart County High School before playing football at Georgia Tech and Furman, where he earned a bachelor's degree in Sociology.

Kenya was heavily influenced by science fiction during his childhood, gravitating towards He-Man, Transformers, Batman, and Star Wars. He also developed a love for video games, particularly fantasy, sports, and action titles.

Kenya's parents, Larry and Dorothy, raised his three siblings and him to value family over possessions, to pursue and apply education, to have a heart for the community, and to honor the God of the Bible.

Kenya has a son, Cameron, and the world's most adorable granddaughter, Hendrix.